The Saint & The Demon

A Novel

t. santitoro
& Ron Sparks

The Saint & The Demon
By t.santitoro & Ron Sparks

Story copyright owned by t.santitoro & Ron Sparks
Cover illustration by t.santitoro
Cover design by Laura Givens

First Printing, January 2024

Hiraeth Publishing
P.O. Box 1248
Tularosa, NM 88352
e-mail: hiraethsubs@yahoo.com

Visit www.hiraethsffh.com for online science fiction, fantasy, horror, scifaiku, and more. Stop by our online bookstore for novels, magazines, anthologies, and collections. **Support the small, independent press...and your First Amendment rights.**

To James B. Baker for his Vision and Generosity, and to Tyree Campbell for his Encouragement,

And also for Bob, Jon and Nic for their Patience, and in Memory of Walt and Alice.

Chapter 1: The Interview Begins

The mosquitoes were just beginning to get annoying and I started looking around for shelter when he finally spoke. A single, simple, sentence so quietly uttered that I almost convinced myself that I had imagined it. Swatting at a buzzing in my ear, I glanced at the old man sitting tranquilly under the tree.

"What was that?" I asked. He sat so still that more than once during the day I had thought he was dead. Irritatingly enough, he was sitting deathly still even now. His damned skin was probably so leathery that he couldn't even feel the pests gnawing on his old bones. Hell - I hadn't wanted to drive this far into the Everglades, surrounded by alligators, snakes, and mosquitoes but my editor had convinced me to do so. There was a story here, she had said: a story worth telling, worth listening to, worth writing. This decrepit old man living in poverty, in a shack in the middle of a swamp, had loved and lost more than any man alive. He was a hero and a villain - a saint and a demon. His untold story was the stuff of fairy tales. Or so I had been told.

His voice rattled behind false teeth as he reiterated his last statement, "I said," and there was an edge to his voice that startled me, "that she always loved the moon on a night like this."

I turned my gaze skyward; the moon was waning and the sky had only a sprinkling of clouds. It hung like a half-eaten cookie opposite the dull glow of the setting sun on the opposite side of the sky. It did look rather remarkable in the twilight. It was an inspiring moon that immediately made me think of my girlfriend, who had just left me.

I must have made a face because the old man laughed softly and slowly turned his head my way. He may be old, I realized, but his eyes were young and fierce. I knew that a once-formidable man was sitting in the chair staring at me. Not just an old man living in the past.

"You know the feeling of love lost, then, do you boy?"

I bristled at his mocking tone, but said nothing. I knew better than to derail the train that had just left the station. The hardest part, the biggest hurdle, had just been passed - he had spoken. Odds were very much in my favor that he would continue speaking if I did nothing to screw this up.

The old man nodded approvingly at my silence. He looked away and stared again at the moon. "I saved her life, you know." His voice was strong and slow as he searched for a way to begin his story. Nodding to himself, he continued. "I saved her life, and in the doing of it I lost my soul."

I looked in sharp surprise at the old man, forgetting for the moment about the pests and sounds of the swamp. Fumbling quietly without taking my eyes from the chair he sat in, I tried to activate the neurosynthetic recorder implanted behind my eyes - standard issue equipment for most reporters nowadays, though mine was a bit dated. I got the feeling that this story was going to be good.

A frail, palsied hand reached up and pointed at the moon. I noticed for the first time that two fingers were missing and angry scars crisscrossed his forearm.

"My most cherished memories are the times when we shared the moon."

I groaned inwardly. This relic was bouncing all over the place. Not keeping a coherent theme from one sentence to the next. He was intelligent - I could see the cunning in his eyes - but he was no storyteller. I knew I would have to guide him through his story and keep him focused.

"Why don't we start from the beginning," I suggested softly. "How did you meet her?"

"Impatient?" The old man chuckled. "Yes, boy, I remember the beginning and I know how to begin. It doesn't come easy, though - the reopening of doors that were closed and locked long ago for good reason. Here," He tossed an enviro-patch to me, "Wouldn't want the mosquitoes to carry you away while I'm telling my story. Put that on while I formulate my thoughts."

Chapter 2: **The Meteor Shower**

Summer, The Near Future

It was almost like a firestorm. Meteorites were streaking through the night sky in a meteor shower like nothing either of them had ever seen before, and here she was, missing it. They'd come up to Lookout Point, for the sole purpose of watching the show but, as usual, Jeff had other ideas.

His right hand was up the back of her sweater, sneakily trying to unfasten her bra, while his left hand slid slowly down her shoulder, around to her chest, his panting breath smelling of the onions he'd had on his pizza half an hour earlier.

Angel sighed and pushed him away. Necking in the jeep might have been ok in their college days, but it seemed a little sophomoric tonight, when her real interest was in what was taking place in the sky. She'd had a bit too much to drink, and was a little light headed, but not enough to give in to Jeff's advances. The night was clear and warm, and they had the top off his jeep. The view would have been great, if he didn't keep getting in her way.

"Knock it off," she told him, trying to see around his bobbing head as he pecked playfully at her neck.

"Oh, come on, Angel. You didn't really get me up here, just to see some lame shooting stars, did you?" Jeff tried to move closer, the jeep's stick shift getting in his way. "Let's make some of our own shooting stars--"

"Quit it!" she said more firmly.

She should have taken her own car. They'd been dating off and on for the past 2 years, and she should have known better. He always pushed for sex, when she really wasn't interested. He was a nice guy, and funny as hell, and she enjoyed his company, but she just couldn't see him as a lover.

Jeff gave up, looking hurt and angry, and heaved a deep sigh. "Ok, look, how 'bout I just take you back to your car?" Typical, thought Angel; he doesn't get what he wants so he wants to go home and pout.

They'd met at the pizza joint on the highway, as usual. They were from different towns, an hour apart in the rural Pennsylvania Mountains, and often drove to the midpoint between their homes to have a pizza and beer together.

They'd met as freshmen several years ago, and had kept in almost constant touch after graduation. They were both from small towns where the local gossip flowed like the area rivers, and the dating prospects were narrowed down to the few people they weren't related to. Thrown together by the lack of other available options, they got along fine as friends, but Jeff wanted something more from their relationship, and Angel was looking for something else entirely.

"What?" she asked, distracted not only by her reverie, but also by the sight of so many meteorites she that couldn't count them. The crescent moon hung low over the mountains, a sliver of silver beneath the streaking sparkles and flares, filling her with an uncommon sense of anticipation - or was it only the beer she'd had?

"Why don't I just take you back for your car?" he repeated dismally.

"Yeah," she answered, her mind on the spectacle, and her feeling of anticipation increased. The shooting stars were so bright they cast their own shadows now. This was definitely a more-than-normal spectacle. "Yeah, ok."

Jeff started the jeep, and they drove the rest of the way back down the mountain to the highway, in silence. Angel watched the sky above them, her mind racing. When they pulled up next to her car, in the parking lot of the pizza place, she gave him a quick peck on the cheek.

"Can I call you next week?" He asked, as she climbed out of his jeep.

Angel hesitated, caught between sympathy for him, and the desire to move on. She opened her mouth to say "sure", but heard herself utter, "Uh, no. I'm going to be busy next week. I'll catch up to you later." Then she turned and jumped into her own 4x4, and drove off, her gaze turning ever upward.

Angel was speeding along the dark country road, and feeling guilty for the way that she'd treated Jeff, when an enormous fireball whizzed by overhead, and struck down in the woods somewhere off to her right. There was a powerful explosion, and she ducked involuntarily, almost careening off the road. She got her SUV under control, and rounded a bend, then inhaled sharply as she stamped on both the break and the clutch, downshifting without thinking.

There, in the middle of the road, was one of the worst accidents she'd ever seen. The black top was strewn with twisted metal engulfed in flame. The parts of at least three different vehicles littered both lanes, and she skidded to a stop, stalling her engine, her mouth agape. From the looks of things, that fireball had impacted right in the road, hitting at least one of the cars, and causing the pile up.

Angel climbed shakily out of her Cherokee, mesmerized by the flames. No one could have survived such complete devastation. Dazed, she walked closer to the scene, wondering what she should do. It was two in the morning, and there was no cell service in this part of the mountains. Unbidden tears came to her eyes as she looked at the devastation.

She heard a groan from the roadside ditch. Someone was alive! Whoever it was, must have been thrown from their car. She shakily climbed over the guardrail. In the light of the towering flames, she spied the crumpled figure of a man. As she moved to approach him, there was another explosion. A screech escaped her throat, as she half slid down the short embankment, to where the man was. He was lying face down, his clothing tattered and singed, his forehead cracked open and bleeding. She had to get him out of there! He groaned when she tried to move him, but she persisted, and finally managed to drag him up the short incline towards the guardrail, tears of frustration burning her eyes. There she paused to catch her breath.

When she looked up, her heart constricted in fear, and a cold chill ran down her spine. The road was full of people! Little dark beings, with large, evil black eyes scurried around the wreckage, darting in and out of the flames, as though impervious to the intense heat.

She ducked down behind the guardrail, and tried to think straight. This couldn't be happening! Who--What! --were those little creatures? With their grey skin, bald heads and huge black eyes, they certainly weren't human. They had to be extraterrestrial. They had to be aliens! The man beside her groaned, and panic gripped her. What was she going to do? If he cried out, he would alert them to her presence. She peered over the guardrail again, uncertain.

The busy little beings were well organized, and methodical, and appeared to be conducting a search. What were they looking for? As she watched, they came across a charred human body. They examined it quickly, then drew some sort of devices, and in a flash of blue radiance, destroyed it.

Angel gulped in a dry mouth. Should she try to get the injured man into the back of her SUV, or wait until the aliens concluded their search and left? What if they found her? Her lips thinned with determination. She had to get herself and the man out of there. If she could get to her car unseen, and get him into the back, perhaps they could escape undetected.

But, when she peaked over the guardrail once more, the aliens were gone!

Angel shook her head to clear it, and looked again. Only the towering flames and wreckage greeted her gaze. She sniffed, the smoke burning her eyes, making them water.

"I must be going crazy," she thought, and then bent back to the unconscious man, the sound of the flames roaring in her ears.

* * *

The man came to on the front seat of her Cherokee. He started violently awake, as if he'd been having a nightmare, a loud gasp escaping him.

"Easy!" she said. "It's ok. You're ok."

He looked around at the unfamiliar surroundings. "Where--?"

"--In my car," she replied before he could finish his question. "There was a crash. You've been injured. I'm taking you to the hospital." The county hospital was the only place she could think to go, though it was quite a distance away. Outside, the dark shapes of trees rushed by, and the lines in the center of the road were a blur.

"NO!" he exploded, and then winced as the outburst caused his head to hammer. "I'm all right," he added, but the hand he'd put to his forehead came away wet and dark with blood.

"You probably need stitches--" Angel began uncertainly, glancing from the road to the stranger. She drew in a sharp breath. Even in the darkness of the SUV, she could see that he was handsome, with piercing, too-pale eyes that almost glowed. Their weird colorization made her feel a bit funny, and she glanced quickly back to the road, her sentence unfinished.

"I'll be fine." he insisted in an even drawl, full of self-confidence. "I just need to get cleaned up."

"Yeah, ok," agreed Angel, still feeling that odd inertia. "We can go to my place."

The stranger grinned, then winced again. "I'm called Cutter. What's your name?"

"Angel." she supplied automatically, before she could stop herself. Ordinarily she didn't give out personal information to people she didn't know. "Angel French."

He rubbed at his wounded temple; closing his odd eyes for a moment, then spoke again. "What actually happened?"

Angel risked another glance in his direction. With his eyes shut, he seemed less confident, a bit vulnerable. "You don't remember?"

"Tell me." he said. He reopened his strange, almost-white eyes, and again she felt an odd urge to comply.

"I'm not sure. A meteor came down in the road back there. There must have been some kind of an accident, there's all kinds of wreckage. Two, maybe three, cars collided. You must have been in one of them."

Cutter heaved a deep sigh, and rested his head back against the seat. They'd crashed? What about the others? He hesitated, and then said, "Did you see anyone

11

else? Besides me? Anyone alive?"

Angel's hands tightened on the steering wheel as she thought of the little grey aliens. "No." she responded, trying to convince herself it had only been her drunken imagination.

Cutter straightened on the seat, directing his piercing gaze at her, his voice hard. "You're lying." he accused levelly.

Angel stammered, her face flushing, again feeling compelled to answer. "I--I--that is--you wouldn't believe me, if I told you--" her voice trailed off, and she gave her attention to her driving, guiding her Cherokee into a right turn that took them off the black top, and onto a narrow dirt road. Thick trees blotted out the overhead sky and its continuing meteor shower.

"Try me." said Cutter, this time his tone was reasonable, almost cajoling.

So Angel told him. She explained about watching the meteors with Jeff, about the anticipation that had washed over her, making her eager to get away, to drive on into the star spangled night, and how she'd come upon the accident, in the middle of the road.

Cutter grinned, his even white teeth flashing in the light of an oncoming vehicle. "Then we were destined to meet."

Angel continued with her story of finding him unconscious in the ditch. When she got to the part about the little grey aliens, Cutter's grin faded, as she'd known it would.

"I--must've had one beer too many--" she offered lamely, expecting him to call her crazy.

But, instead, he demanded in a tight hiss, "How many of them were there?"

"Ten or fifteen I suppose." She answered, but wondered why he'd want to know. He sounded as if he actually believed her insane tale.

The approaching car pulled closer, almost along side of them on the narrow dirt road, and Angel gave her full attention to keeping her Cherokee out of the ditch. Beside her, Cutter was silent and watchful, almost tense.

When the other vehicle had passed, he said, "Did

the greys see you?"

"No. I hid behind the guardrail. When I looked up--
they'd disappeared. No sound, no movement. They were
just--gone! As if they were never even there. Which, of
course they weren't. I don't know; I must have hit my
head, when I skidded, or something. "

After all, everyone knew there was no such thing as
aliens.

Chapter 3: Truth and Lies

The old man sat back with a heavy sigh of reminiscence, his keen eyes reflecting a bit of pain, and he spoke in a hard-edged voice.

"Angel had no way of knowing, of course, that I had already been running from the greys for some time."

I rubbed my eyes to rid myself of the double images. An unfortunate side effect of early-model recorders was soreness, redness, and irritation of the eyes. The old man seemed content to wait me out. He was apparently not unfamiliar with the plight of modern-day journalists.

As I flushed my eyes with a special saline-like solution, the obvious discrepancies in the old man's story came to the forefront of my mind. He was lying, obviously, on a number of accounts. How to deal with it, though, was somewhat of an ambiguous issue.

I could allow him to continue his story unabated. If I did that, the old fart would probably go further into the looking glass and shortly his tale would be complete fantasy. I wasn't sure if this was the story my editor had sent me out here to get. She was an unforgiving bitch who would castrate me in front of the other journalists to send home a lesson on the price of failure.

On the other hand, I could call the old man out on his story here and now. There were certain elements to his story that were simply fascinating, but they were all wrapped in the fairy tale and getting at them would be difficult. How to separate the truth from the lie? My questioning might send the recluse back into hiding. I couldn't bear the thought of trying to wait him out in the middle of the night. Even with the enviro-patch, the insects and sounds of the night were quite frankly frightening to me. Miami was my city - a true metropolis and not some backwater hut in a swamp.

My choice was simple and I made it quickly. A journalist was a seeker of truth. I would confront the lies and banish them with a wave of my virtual pen. I would have to call the old man out and live with the consequences.

"I have a couple of questions," I began, "clarifications really, that I would like to ask you before we continue."

The old man grunted his assent with a nod of his head.

"The meteor shower," I ventured, "The one that rained death on a Pennsylvania freeway. Are you referring to the The Great Meteor Disaster?"

The Great Meteor Disaster was validation for every Chicken Little, the-sky-is-falling, doomsayer in the world. NASA's Near-Earth Object Program at JPL hadn't caught so much as a peep from their satellites about the incoming disaster. In the middle of the night, death had rained from the skies along the Northeastern United States.

Nine states were affected, but Pennsylvania was hardest hit by far. Five thousand men, women, and children were never heard from again. Hundreds were vaporized so completely by the impact of the meteors that no trace of them was ever found again.

In the chaotic aftermath, no explanation was sufficient. Lagging public interest and national funding of the Space Program was revitalized by the event. No expense was spared as a fleet of orbital weapons was put in space to combat any such future threat. It was a worldwide wakeup call that was very seriously heeded.

The old man nodded slowly, a mischievous twinkle in his eyes. *He knows what's coming, the wily bastard.*

"The Great Meteor Disaster," I stated slowly and simply, "happened seven years ago."

"I can do the math," the old man groused. "Ask your damned questions and be done with them." He waggled a liver-spotted finger at me in admonishment, "I don't have so much time left in me that I want to play word games with you, boy."

I felt my face flush with anger at his patronizing tone. "Fine," I snapped and drove right to the point. "You talk of yourself as a young man in your story, but seven years ago you were hardly young. You, sir, are an old man."

The old man grinned with a mouth only half-filled with teeth. "Yes! Ask me direct and do not dance around

15

the subject. You are not half as smart as you think you are, boy. Word games will only confuse you."

I ground my teeth and counted to ten before I replied, resisting the urge to get up and leave.

"How old," I enunciated carefully, "are you?"

"Thirty-one."

I sat back and looked in exasperation at the moon above us. Typical Florida nights called for clouds to move in and hang ominously over the land. True to form, the slow buildup was evident in the ring the moon was projecting in the clouds as they formed. Soon, the moon would be obscured completely from view. Kind of like the truth here and now.

I was tired of being insulted by this old man. He wanted directness? I would give it to him.

"You are a liar." Simple. Powerful.

Slowly, the old man turned his head and looked directly at me. For the first time, I felt the full force of his gaze and was momentarily taken aback by it. His colorless eyes drilled into mine with an intensity I knew I could never match. In the end, like a lesser beast, I was forced to look away.

"Yes," whispered the old man savagely, "I am a liar when it suits me. One of the all-time greats I imagine. I have also been a killer, a murderer, a savior, and a Good Samaritan."

He turned his gaze away from me, for which I was instantly grateful, and continued. "I like you, boy. I like your anger and self-righteousness. You are so full of yourself and life that I love being here near you. I can feel your life, you know. I can feel your essence and it burns, hot and fierce, around you. It embraces you and flows through you.

"I had such a fire within me only a few short years ago. I was young and powerful." A weathered hand reached up and touched his forehead, "I knew I was going to live forever. There was nothing I could not, would not, do for the right reason. And there is, at the end of it all, only one reason worth such dedication and devotion in all this world." He looked keenly at me again and I shifted uncomfortably, "Do you know what that reason is, boy?"

I sighed and tried to act indifferent, although I was again being drawn into his hypnotic eyes, "I don't know. Happiness?"

An old hand slapped the arm of his chair with the sharp sound of a gunshot, "No! Happiness means nothing in and of itself. Happiness, true happiness is not possible without Love, boy. Wealth, power, health - they are all worthless attributes without Love."

I didn't miss the capital "L." Once again, this story was starting to get interesting - but I was no closer to the truth. The old man was right; it was pretty much pointless to play word games with him. He very evidently had the ability to outmaneuver me.

He sensed my defeatism and softened his tone. He wanted to tell his story and no personality clash was going to stop him. "I know you have questions boy. You don't know it yet, but my apparent age is the least of them. Little grey aliens are not the crucial aspect of this story."
He sat back in his chair, "Indeed, boy, even the fact that I myself am not Human has little bearing in light of what this story is really about - Love."

I sat back in shock, speechless, as the old man once again continued his narration.

Chapter 4: Jealous Passions

Angel sat on the front porch of her small cabin, comfortable in her favorite Adirondack chair. The sound of the shower running just reached her beneath the louder cacophony of the woodland birds.

The sun was up, barely cresting the mountains, and soft light flooded the porch where she sat with her dog Asti at her feet.

She was lost in contemplation, occasionally patting the lab's broad head, her mind occupied with the strange events of the last few hours. The frightening revelation that humans were not alone in the universe, was overshadowed by the even more ominous possibility that she was no longer in control of her own actions. Against her better judgment, she'd brought a complete stranger into her home, when she should have driven him to the county hospital. She lived alone on the outskirts of town, and never entertained, so bringing Cutter here had been completely out of character. The weird thing was, she felt none of the nervousness, guilt or paranoia she ought to be feeling. Instead, the events of the past few hours had left her exhausted yet oddly exhilarated.

Her reverie was rudely interrupted as Asti jumped up, barking frantically at the sound of an approaching vehicle. She glanced up, startled to recognize a familiar jeep bumping up her rutted driveway.

The Wrangler pulled up before her porch, stopped, and a figure jumped out.

"Jeff!" she stood, confused by his sudden appearance. "What are you doing here?" He'd been to her house only once before, when he'd given her a lift home, after her old car had broken down.

He came to the bottom step of the log porch, his youthful boy-next-door features looking tense and drawn. "I was worried about you. I tried calling a few times, but the cell service's out--"

"Worried?" she parroted, not following. Bad phone service was nothing new out here.

"I didn't know if you'd made it home last night, or

not. What with all the accidents and fires--"

Angel put a hand to her forehead, feeling like she was coming out of a dream. What was Jeff going on about? What fires? The only accident she knew about was the one she'd come across, on the way home.

"Haven't you heard?" Jeff's face registered his disbelief as he stood at the bottom step, looking up at her with puzzled eyes. "Where've you been? It's all over the news and Internet--Who's *he*?" He interrupted himself with a surprised start.

Angel spun around to see Cutter, standing in the doorway, clad only in a towel, his pale hair wet and tousled. It was her first good look at him. In the growing sunlight, his tightly muscled body was as close to her idea of male perfection as she could ever imagine. His skin was darkly bronzed, as if he spent a lot of time in the sun, and his flaxen spiked hair was sun bleached. The only flaws were the large gash across his temple, and the demanding question in his pale eyes.

Angel caught her breath at the sight of him, then let it go slowly, turning back to Jeff. She said with casual evenness, "It's Cutter. Cutter, this is Jeff--a friend of mine."

Jeff's features darkened slightly at her description of him as simply a "friend", but he didn't correct her. "Cutter?" he scoffed at the odd name. "Cutter Who?"

"Cutter Steele." she replied automatically, without thinking, even though she didn't have the slightest notion of Cutter's real surname. Cutter said nothing, watching the interplay between them. He grinned easily at Jeff's discomfiture, and leaned in the doorway as if he owned the place, challenging Jeff's presence.

The moment turned awkward; the silence dragged. Angel knew what Jeff must be thinking, the wrong conclusions he must be making, but somehow she felt no need to explain. After a few long moments, she ventured, "What were you saying, Jeff? What's all over the news?"

Jeff struggled to shift his attention back to her, away from the handsome stranger, his unexpected competition. "Huh? Oh! The meteor shower! You know how meteors usually burn up entering the atmosphere?

19

Well, during last night's shower, hundreds of them didn't burn up! They made landfall, all across the country, causing all kinds of damage. Some of 'em hit our area. They're estimating something like 4500 dead! That's why I was afraid maybe you'd been in an accident. Especially when I couldn't get you on the phone--Apparently you're alright." he finished pointedly, glaring once more at Cutter.

Cutter came out onto the porch then, and threw an arm around Angel's shoulders, his cocky grin widening. "She's just fine." he remarked smoothly.

Angel knew she should have felt resentment at this uninvited and possessive attitude, but she didn't. Instead, she detected a warm glow flooding her senses. She said to Jeff, "It was nice of you to come all the way over here, Jeff, but really, I'm OK. *We're* alright."

Jeff nodded curtly, getting the picture. "Sure." he said. "Well, I'd better go." And he turned and got back into his jeep, started it, and drove away, banging the gears.

Something deep within Angel cried out in sympathy for Jeff, but the warm glow washing over her completely drowned it out.

* * *

Cutter dressed in the small bedroom of Angel's log cabin, pulling on the new clothes she'd brought back from town. His own apparel had been almost completely scorched in last night's accident. His thoughts centered mostly on Angel, blocking out any other invading memories of last night, and he dressed quickly, eager to be with her.

He found her extremely attractive, and seriously considered the probability that she might be The One. Circumstances had brought them together, and there was no denying the physical attraction they felt for each other. He finished dressing, and went back out into the living area, where he was immediately rewarded by Angel's positive response to his new appearance.

She grinned, eying him rather lewdly. The faded jeans and black tee shirt fit just tightly enough, allowing her to appreciate all of his natural attributes fully. "Nice." she commented. "Kinda makes me glad your other clothes got ruined." The things he'd been wearing when she'd found him in the ditch had been non-descript and rather utilitarian, a far cry from the way he looked now, wearing clothes which she found far more attractive. Her smile brightened, then faded, as she thought of last night's accident, and the reports she'd just been watching concerning the event.

Jeff had been right. Word of the disaster was all over the news, and the general public was being inundated by media coverage. But there was something about the news reports of the incident, which bothered Angel. Something she couldn't quite put her finger on. In town, when she'd been shopping for Cutter's clothes, it had been so clear to her. But now, here, in front of Cutter, she couldn't seem to remember what it was.

Cutter basked in her approval of his new look, aware that his attraction to her was being mirrored by her own response. He let his pale eyes wander up and down her petite figure, taking in her dark skin and black hair, his desire to be with her suddenly so intense he had to turn away.

Not yet! he told himself firmly. *Be patient.* She didn't even know who he was, after all. They were strangers.

Angel watched him turn away, disappointed that he hadn't returned her flirting. As soon as his eyes left her, however, her mind cleared, and she recalled what it was about the news coverage of the meteor shower that had bothered her. With all of the reports she'd seen and listened to all day, not one had mentioned aliens or little grey people.

She said carefully, "Cutter, I think I'm the only one who saw those aliens, last night."

He spun back to her, his face hard. Why was she bringing up the greys? He'd put them out of his mind, and didn't want to think of them right now. There were other, more important, matters he needed to address. He said, "Does it matter? They're gone."

Angel opened her mouth to protest his attitude, but felt herself weakening under his gaze. She forced herself to say, "What if they come back?"

21

Cutter turned away again, releasing her from his penetrating stare, hiding his own fear. What if they did come back?? What if they found him before he could--

"They won't." He replied harshly, more to convince himself, than her.

Again free of his glare, Angel re-gathered her self-confidence enough to say to his back, "How do *you* know? Cutter, how do you *know?*"

For a long moment, he didn't say anything, the silence filled with the sounds of birds outside, emphasizing the quiet, and he just stared out the cabin's front window, considering. How much should he tell her? How much did she really need to know? Finally, he sighed and said, "Because I know them. They've been after me for a long time."

* * *

"I don't believe it."

The summer sun was setting, now, going down behind the mountain ridge, off to their right, and the crickets and leaf bugs were beginning their nightly chorus. Angel's dog Asti was off chasing rabbits somewhere, leaving them alone on the porch. Angel sat with her back against Cutter's chest in a wooden love seat, trying to digest all that he'd just told her about himself.

Cutter stirred, his body stiffening. " I don't see how you can so easily accept the existence of the greys, and yet deny the possibility that other off-worlders might also exist."

His tone clearly betrayed his anger, and Angel sat forward, away from his tensed body, and turned to look into his pale, almost-white eyes.

"You're telling me you're an alien! Just like those--those--little grey---"

"*Not* like them!" thundered Cutter, wincing inwardly at her insult, his jaw hard. "I told you: they're genocidal monsters, bent on destroying my people." He hadn't told her everything, but what he had told her was true. That he was from another world, millions of light years away, and that the greys were his enemies. That they'd been chasing him--and others like him--since his birth, determined to kill him. To wipe out every last one of his people, his entire race.

But Angel didn't appear to understand. She was in denial, unable to view Cutter as someone as alien as those little grey creatures with the energy weapons. He looked so human--

She said, "Don't you think we humans would have known if aliens had been visiting us for the last few centuries?"

Cutter heaved an impatient sigh. "We've been trained from birth to fit into your society. I'm as 'American' as you are, Angel! I just never actually lived here. I spent my childhood in sheltered tunnels, hiding from detection by the greys, studying your culture. Preparing. Hoping for a chance to come here and disappear." He pulled her back against him again, and put his arms around her, then continued. "I just want to be as free as you are. To live my life without the constant threat of attack. The greys wouldn't've left, if they'd thought I was alive. They must have assumed I died in the crash. I'm free of them. Now let's just forget about it, OK? They're gone."

Angel settled back against his chest, an odd feeling of contentment washing over her as she felt him, too, relax. She was aware of his heart--an alien heart! --beating against her, drumming an even tattoo, not unlike her own pulse.

Shortly, their close contact quickened his heartbeat. She turned in his arms, to gaze once more into his colorless eyes. Their gazes locked, Cutter's hard and unwavering and demanding; Angel's soft and yielding. She initiated a kiss, which he responded to immediately, fiercely. Aroused, his breath quickened, and his hands began to explore her body. Angel felt her own desire awaken. A desire she had not known she possessed. A passion Jeff had never stirred. She drew Cutter's face to her own, kissed him again--

--And then he pulled away, panting, barely in control of himself, his face twisted in self-denial.

"----I can't!" He moaned, his eyes closed, pushing her gently away. "Angel-----you don't understand. I can't----"

"It's OK," she whispered. "Come on. We both want

23

to----"

He gulped, trying to control a raging urgency. "No, I'm----not like human males. If we--if we're ---together---we'll have a permanent hormonal Bonding to each other." He opened his eyes, but did not look at her. Until now, he'd allowed himself to influence her. Using a power inherent in his kind, he'd permitted his gaze to fall upon her, pushing His Will into her subconscious. But now was the time for him to refrain. To allow *her* free will to decide. This had to be purely her decision, her own choice. "We'll be Pair Bonded; life mates. You must understand-----"

"I do." she said gently, caressing him with soft fingers, attempting to soothe his distress.

"*No*. You don't!"

The desperation in his voice snapped her out of her lustful state, her full attention all at once focused on what he was saying.

"If we mate, Angel, you will have power over my very life. If you ever leave me, I will die. Literally. My body will wither and I will *die*. You have to understand this! It's important. I'll die if you leave! You must be certain. You have to know if this is what you want. I'm not human--"

Angel silenced him with another long, passionate kiss.

Chapter 5: The Good Life

Still Summer, In The Near Future

Fox Walters walked out of the music shop with a gig bag over his left shoulder and a swagger in his step. The money Boomer had given him was nearly gone, but he had a new guitar, and he knew it wouldn't be long before he'd be playing lead for some rock band. It was the fastest way to pick up girls, and not a bad way to earn some cash.

He crossed the busy Philadelphia street, and a man on the opposite corner caught his eye. The man was tall, with pale, spiked blond hair, and for just a moment, he reminded Fox of someone. His steps faltered, but he caught himself, and continued on, a trace of guilt and sadness lingering in his thoughts. His best friend was dead. The crash that had claimed him, had almost taken Fox's life as well. He was barely 20, full of the vigor of self-preservation, and had been quicker to exit the vehicle than his friend had been. When they had impacted, he'd been the first one out of the wreck. His friend had stayed to help some of the others who were trapped, and had become trapped himself. The enemy had been right behind, and it had been Fox who'd ordered the rest to disburse, leaving the wounded as a diversion. His best friend had been one of those wounded.

That the others had taken his orders was not a surprise. He was the kind of person whom people just naturally followed. Given time, Fox Walters knew he would lead them all. It was in his genetic make up, his dynamic personality, and his charismatic way with people. Sure, it bothered him now, that he'd had to leave his best friend behind, but at the time, he'd made the decision as easily as breathing. He'd been born to command, and the mission was far more important than any single operative.

It was just toward sunset, the summer evening humid, and the day's heat was still reflecting off of the paving and buildings. He reached the other side of the street, and headed for the small studio apartment he'd rented with some of Boomer's money. The man on the corner turned as he passed, and Fox re-adjusted his gig bag, wary of being robbed, and then deliberately lengthened his stride. He'd learned early on that one could never be too sure, on the streets of Philadelphia.

He'd chosen this city for just that reason. It was a place where anyone could disappear, where newcomers were not questioned, and being different was hardly noticed. And Fox Walters certainly was "different".

As a member of the elite colonization team that had been sent to settle and breed on Earth, Fox was both a warrior and a lover. He'd been trained in every style of martial arts, as well as in the art of making love. He knew how to fight, and fight well, but the most urgent part of his mission was to procreate. He was here to hunt for a life mate and to impregnate her with his seed as soon as possible. The seed of a new race of half-humans. To both expedite this goal and make a living on this new world, he felt that his best chances were along the lines of becoming a rock star.

Fox had learned a lot about rock stars, while studying human customs. Rock stars were sought after by the public, and adored by admiring groupies. Male members of rock groups were frequently inundated by hoards of female fans. Fox was a talented musician who could play rock rifts from Pink Floyd, Odd Man Out, Tomfoolery, and the Who, as well as perform classical pieces. He was handsome in a scruffy way, and was considered good looking on his home world. Doubt about whether the human women would agree, never even entered his mind. That he had the arrogance to complete his plan of rock stardom was never in question. And it certainly didn't occur to him that his brash attitude just might get him into trouble on this alien world.

***

It was a gorgeous summer afternoon. The sunlight was bright, but the air temperature was only in the low eighties with a slight breeze, the crowds of tourists comfortable in their lightweight clothes.

Angel French strolled beside Cutter Steele, window-shopping on Main Avenue in quaint downtown Hawley,

PA. Tourist season was in full swing, and the uneven slate sidewalks were full of shoppers looking for antique bargains and crafts. Cutter's posture was a little tense, and Angel could feel his discomfiture. At home in her cabin, he'd exuded his usual, strong self-confidence, but here in the middle of 'small town USA', he seemed preoccupied and nervous. She saw his features reflected in the storefront before them, and noticed the way his eyes constantly darted over the crowd, restless.

She held his arm, her dark hand twined around his muscular bicep, and looked up, studying his expression. "What is it?" she asked, as they stood before an old-fashioned ice cream parlor.

Cutter grinned uneasily. "Nothing. Why?"

"I don't know, you seem—nervous."

Steele glanced warily around at the mobs of tourists filling the walkways. He shrugged.

Angel's brows pulled into a slight frown. The last weeks with Cutter had been ideal, getting to know each other in the comfortable familiarity of her cabin. They'd talked and made love until words were unnecessary, and they'd seemed to be made for each other. But today something was different. The man she thought she'd begun to know was surprising her with his unexpected behavior. Maybe he was just anxious over the new surroundings. He was, after all, a stranger here.

She said, "Want to buy some ice cream?"

"Ice cream? What's that?" He'd seen commercials, back home, and was aware that it was something to consume, but there'd been no way to know exactly what kind of food those advertisements were offering.

"Come on." She pulled his arm, and they went into the shop. They entered the shadowed coolness of the small parlor, and crossed the creaking wooden floor to the counter. Below the serving bar, and extending along its length, was a well-lit freezer containing buckets of frozen, different-colored substances. "Pick a flavor," said Angel.

Cutter grinned again, his conduct suddenly reverting to the one with which Angel had become familiar. He said firmly, "You choose."

Angel scanned the names above the ice cream

buckets, and then spoke to the waitress. "Ok. Hmmmm... Let's see...I'll have a double-dip vanilla cone, and my friend here will have peanut butter ripple."

The young woman took Angel's money, gave her some change, scooped out their order, and handed them their cones with a smile. "Have a nice day."

As they headed for the exit, Angel licked at her cone. Cutter watched, and then copied her action. His eyes suddenly widened, and he gasped, almost choking in surprise.

"It's hot!" he exclaimed loudly. "I mean, cold! It—it sort of burns!" Around them, people turned and stared.

Angel rolled her dark eyes and grinned widely. She said to the other patrons, "He's-- foreign. Never had ice cream before." The other people grinned back, delighted with his reaction to their frozen American snack.

Outside, Cutter's mood suddenly became tense again. He licked at his ice cream, enjoying its flavor, but Angel could sense that he was again uncomfortable. She said, "Let's walk over to the park."

They strolled together down the sidewalk, passing various shops and galleries, crossed the railroad tracks and bridge, and then made a right into the park. Children were playing on the playground equipment, their parents watching from benches under the trees. Angel led Cutter to the bandstand pavilion, and took a place on the empty steps, where he joined her, immediately beginning to relax.

She gave her attention to her melting ice cream, and then feigning indifference, said, "You're kinda different today."

Cutter didn't look at her. He licked a long white drip off his bronzed hand, and scanned the park, with a soft sigh. He said, "Yeah."

"What's up?"

Now his eyes met hers, and then darted quickly away. He said softly, "This—is all so different, Angel."

"What do you mean, 'different'?" She finished her snack, and regarded him seriously.

"From—from my home world."

She thought about that for a moment. Cutter

wasn't just some out-of-towner, some New Yorker, or someone from another country. He was from a whole other world. As always, the thought struck her almost dumb with amazement. She stuttered. "T—tell me."

His jaw tightened for an instant, then slackened again. Should he tell her? Would she think him weak? He finished his cone, and gestured toward their surroundings. "It's so—open." Not at all like the tunnels he'd grown up in. He felt dangerously exposed in the embrace of the low, two- and three-storied Victorian buildings lining the streets, and even worse in the vast parkland, with its vaulted blue sky above them. Sitting here beneath the domed ceiling of the pavilion, however, he felt a little less vulnerable, but even this was still a more unprotected environment that what he was used to.

Angel nodded with understanding. He'd described his childhood living quarters to her before, but she'd never realized until now, how being outside might affect him. She said, "Want to go home?"

Cutter didn't even consider the possibility. His jaw clenched again, and he shook his head. He wanted to acclimate himself to this world, to this life. When he spoke, his voice was the firm tone to which Angel had grown accustomed. "No."

***

The stars were just beginning to come out, when Cutter and Angel left the diner on Main Avenue, just after their supper. The crowds of tourists were dispersing, cars pulling away from the metered parking spaces along the street. They walked in step, Angel happily content, and Cutter more comfortable under the broad arch of darkening sky, than he had been beneath the noonday blaze.

It had been a perfect day. They had shopped and supped, and walked and talked. As darkness fell, and they strode back to Angel's SUV, she happened to glance up at the sky. The moon had risen and hung, like a shining sliver of melon, upon the backdrop of blackness. Her arm wrapped around Cutter's, she said, "Look. Isn't that beautiful?"

Cutter followed the direction of her gaze, and his

29

lips pulled into a slow smile. He patted her hand, so delicate on his arm, and replied, "Until I came here, I'd never seen such beauty. I'll always think of you when I see it. Of how even more beautiful you are."

Angel blushed, giving him a push with her free hand. "Get real!"

"I'm serious!"

"Didn't you say your home world has three moons?" She demanded, diverting his attention away from the flattery.

"Yes, but they're very small, and none of us have ever seen any of them in person. Not in my lifetime, anyway." They reached the Cherokee, and stood, still looking up at the sky, and he continued. "Between the grey's constant strafing, and the necessity of our having to stay in the tunnels, we rarely got an opportunity to watch the sky, let alone spot any of the moons."

Angel didn't know what to say. She'd always taken the moon, and sight of it, for granted.

Finally she said, "Well, I'm glad we can share this one, then."

Cutter drew her closer, and kissed her forehead lightly. "Yes, at least we can do that. No matter where we each are on this world, we'll always look up at the same moon. It'll always connect us."

"Whoa!" exclaimed Angel. "Are you planning on going somewhere?"

He hesitated. "Yes. In a few days. But I won't be gone long. You know I can't be. Our hormonal bond would prevent it. But, I need to contact some of my people."

"Why?" He'd led her to believe that he'd intended to blend into human society and forget his past.

Cutter sighed, opening the passenger door, and getting in. Angel remained standing by the driver's side, the door ajar. "Cutter, why?"

At first he said nothing. Then his voice came from the car's interior, subdued but firm.

"Because I've been given the name of the district coordinator, and I'm expected to contact him, to let him know that I'm alive. That I made it."

"Why alone? Why can't I go with you?"

"Angel, get in." he said sounding impatient.

"No. Answer me, Cutter. Why can't I go with you?"

"Because—because it might be dangerous." There. He'd said it. He hadn't wanted to worry her, but she'd demanded an answer, and he'd given it.

"Dangerous?" Now she did get into the SUV, closing the door, her face twisted into lines of concern.

"The greys will be watching. Waiting. Searching for any sign of our presence. I don't want you in the middle of anything, Angel." He indicated the stars. "If you could see what they've done to our home, you'd understand--." His throat constricted, and he cut himself off, suddenly sounding miserable.

Angel moved closer to him, barely avoiding the stick shift in the darkened vehicle. She said in a soft voice, "That's not your home!"

He gave her a puzzled look. "What do you mean?"

She took his hand, and placed it over her heart. "Here's your home, Cutter Steele."

He cupped her breast a moment, then slid his arms around her small shoulders and kissed her tenderly, and a feeling of peace descended upon him. But, somehow, he knew it was only a temporary peace.

***

Fox helped unload the instruments from the back of a beat-up white van, grinning to himself. He'd auditioned for a band two days ago, had been readily and eagerly accepted, and already he was preparing for a gig. He'd be playing with a local Philly band, Tomfoolery, and they'd be opening up for a much more well known group called Odd Man Out. Fox would be filling in for an absentee band member, but Tomfoolery only had two roadies, so he was also doubling as a roadie.

The sun of an alien world beat down upon his back as he hefted some equipment, but the sweat dripping down his forehead did nothing to sour his mood. The blue sky was something he hadn't been used to, but living off the Philadelphia streets for a number of days, before connecting with Boomer, had desensitized him to the outdoors. Now he found that he was actually enjoying

31

what folks in these parts referred to as "summer weather". The warm breeze felt better than the moist, stale cavern air he'd always known, and the grey clouds drifting across the sun were a welcome addition to his catalogue of new experiences.

"Hey, Fox! Hurry up, man." One of the roadies gave him a scowl, a cigarette dangling from his down-turned mouth. "You gonna stand there gapin' at the clouds, or help me get this shit indoors?" They were standing at the loading dock of the First Union Arena, in Scranton, Pennsylvania, and he was eager to help the band get everything set up for tonight's concert. The breeze had picked up, pushing dark clouds before it, promising rain later. Better to get everything indoors as soon as possible.

Fox silently cursed the impatient man. Someday, when he and his race were in control of things, people like this roadie were going to be sorry. He shrugged off the other's nasty mood, knowing that eventually even people as famous as the band members themselves would be looking up to him with awe.

The roadie stubbed out his cigarette on the baking-hot black top of the parking lot, said, "You can bring in the microphone stands when you're done there."

He gave the roadie an even glare, and then in a low, firm voice, said, "Say please."

The other stuttered, paling under Fox's powerful gaze and undeniable Will. "P-please."

Fox grinned, and turned away, releasing him. Humans were so easy. Not that he was usually one to push them around, but sometimes he just couldn't help himself.

"That's better." He said, and continued to unload the van.

***

Jeff Kowalski shook his head and, beneath the edge of his protective helmet, beads of sweat flew from his soaked hair to spray across the boxing ring. He closed in on his sparing partner, not seeing the familiar dark skin and crooked nose but, instead, a tall, blond man with an arrogant expression.

He'd been thinking of nothing else, but Cutter

Steele, since he'd met the cocky son-of-a-bitch at Angel's cabin. Cutter Steele, who'd moved in on his territory, charming Angel with his blond good looks and aloof manner. He ground his plastic teeth guards together at just the thought.

What did Steele have, that he didn't? His own body was powerfully built and muscular from his recreational weight lifting and kick boxing. Sure, he had a scar or two, but that only added character, didn't it? And besides, Steele himself had been sporting a good scar, that day on the porch of Angel's cabin, so he knew she wasn't adverse to physical flaws. So what was it that drew her to the blond stranger?

Whatever it was, he wanted to pound it out of Steele. He wanted to bash the bastard's face in. He slugged his sparing partner aggressively, still seeing the blond man on Angel's front porch, and felt a brief sense of satisfaction. But he knew, deep inside, that he'd never feel any true satisfaction until he could batter the real Cutter Steele.

***

The crowd was getting agitated. Backstage, Fox could hear the roar building, as the seats out front filled with people. This would be an important performance. In the middle of their Prisoner of the Mind World Tour, Odd Man Out had taken time to come here, to the middle of rural Pennsylvania, to do a show benefiting those people who had been so utterly devastated by the Meteor Shower. As concertgoers streamed into the arena, the crescendo became almost overwhelming, and Fox grinned at Tomfoolery's drummer, who tossed his head at the noise of excitement, and grinned back. In less than an hour, the set would begin, and Fox could feel his heart pounding in anticipation. He knew the music well, had played it ceaselessly back home, and had no doubts about his ability to stay with the beat, yet his desire to play before the audience wasn't as great as the nervousness which suddenly gripped him. This anxiety was a new feeling, something he wasn't accustomed to. He glanced over at the lead guitarist, who was tuning his Gibson, and the other looked up. They exchanged a thumbs up, and Fox

33

bent to tune his own guitar.

***

Their seats in the balcony were sheltered and almost private, despite the enormous crowd, and Angel watched Cutter closely, to get his reaction. This was the first time they'd been among so many people, the first time he'd agreed to attend a public function.

She'd asked him to attend the concert, several days ago, before she'd learned of his discomfort outdoors.

"It's a benefit for the victims of the Meteor Shower," she'd told him, eager to attend the event. "And my favorite bands—Tomfoolery and Odd Man Out—will both be playing."

Cutter had shrugged indifferently and accepted her invitation. But now, in the midst of so many humans, she wondered how it must feel to him, to be so alone. So outnumbered. Then she suddenly laughed aloud, as the irony struck her. She was one of the few African Americans in the entire arena; she ought to know how Cutter was feeling!

Cutter turned at her giggle. "Having a good time?"

She squeezed his arm. "I always have a good time, when I'm with you, Cutter Steele. How 'bout you? You ok?"

He grinned his best arrogant grin. "Never better."

***

Fox was riding high on the elation of having performed with Tomfoolery before a live audience. Odd Man Out was still onstage, and the drum beat vibrated through him, as he packed away his guitar, and began loading the white van. He'd been hoping to connect with Boomer again. The district coordinator had left a message for him on the Resistance Website message board, stating his desire to attend the concert, and Fox had hoped to see him here.

Ah well. He shrugged off his disappointment. Someone had to run the resistance, and all that that entailed. He knew that, all too soon, it would be him making all the decisions, coordinating the arrival of the new operatives, and keeping things going smoothly. Before he knew it, there'd be no time for music. He might as well enjoy it while he could.

He finished loading the equipment into the van, and went back into the building, only to be surprised by a large mob of female groupies. Yeah, this was the life.

***

The concert had been fantastic. As Jeff Kowalski moved down the steep arena steps towards an exit, his concentration on his footing, he mentally reviewed the reasons for his enjoyment. Odd Man Out had expertly played most of his favorite songs, and Tomfoolery had given an equally excellent performance. They were two of Angel's favorite bands, and he scowled inwardly at the notion that they would probably have attended the concert together, had they still been seeing each other.

He'd left the boxing ring in the gym late that afternoon, after an exhausting workout, and had then gone home to shower and dress for the concert. He'd briefly considered asking one of the girls from work to go with him, but had nixed the idea almost immediately. The bands were Angel's favorites, and it just wouldn't seem right to hear them with anyone else.

He picked his way down the stairs, following the departing crowd, and around the level landing where souvenirs were being sold. He was almost to the exit, when something caught his attention. A familiar shape, an intimate laugh.

He stopped cold, the mob of people forced to move around him, like creek water around a stone. Ahead, just to the right of a support pillar, stood Angel. And she was not alone.

***

Angel was wearing a coral colored tank top and faded blue jeans, both of which enhanced her dark coloring, and she looked as fresh and lovely as ever. Jeff watched her, unable to move, all of his attention focused on her beautiful figure. He wanted to hide, and just stare at her, at every gesture, every movement she made. Burn the vision of her into his eyes and memory. Before he could rouse himself into action, however, she turned and spotted him.

"Jeff!" She sounded surprised, but her features

35

betrayed her pleasure at seeing him again.

"I should have known you'd be here, too!"

"Er—yeah." There was nothing for it now, but to go over and talk to her, even with Steele standing there. He approached them, reluctantly including the blond man in his gaze. Steele was wearing a multi-colored tie-dyed shirt that reminded Jeff of a bull's eye, the center of the design, just about where the man's heart should be, and he narrowed his eyes. If only he had heat-ray vision or something...

"Great concert, huh?" said Steele, with real enthusiasm and an easy grin.

"Yeah," said Jeff again, followed by a long silence.

The moment turned awkward and Angel said, "Where've you been keeping yourself?"

"At the gym mostly." Said Kowalski. "You know, working out. Kick boxing." He added the second in a pointed manner, for Steele's benefit.

Cutter's grin widened, unperturbed by the veiled threat. He put an arm around Angel, said, "Well, if we want to beat the traffic, we'd better get going, Angel. See ya around," he threw at Jeff, and moved her smoothly away, toward the exit.

Jeff stood watching them depart, his hands clenched into white-knuckled fists, his breathing slow and deep, his eyes shooting imaginary darts into the bulls-eye design on Steele's broad back.

"Do you know that man?"

Kowalski turned to see a big blond man with a beard and dark sunglasses. He was dressed in a slate grey suit with a white shirt and charcoal tie. Not the usual rock fan attire.

"What the hell business is it of yours?" he grumped back, annoyed.

"I've been following him." Explained the large stranger from behind his dark glasses. He spoke with a slight accent that Jeff could not identify with any certainty as either British or Australian. "He looks like the man who ran off with my wife and my –quite sizable—bank account."

"What?" Kowalski suddenly grinned. How

interesting.

"I tracked them to your local airport, and have been looking all over for them. Do you happen to know his name?"

"Yeah, it's 'Cutter Steele'."

"Has he been in town long?"

"No. Showed up just after the Meteor Shower."

"That would be about right. They caught a plane to this country a few days before the disaster. Would you also know where he's residing?"

Jeff's grin widened. This was getting good. "Sure. He's living with my ex-girlfriend."

Although his eyes were hidden, the big man's face looked grim. "I don't want to alarm you, but that man is dangerous. This isn't the first time he's gotten away with this. He claims to be a foreigner, in need of a place to stay, and winds up taking women for everything they've got, before they end up disappearing. I don't know what he's done with my wife, but I intend to find out. Could I have your ex-girlfriend's address? Maybe even some directions?"

"I can do better than that," said Jeff. "She lives up in the mountains above Lake Wallenpaupack, in the middle of nowhere, but I can show you exactly where she lives."

The big man glanced at his watch. "Alright. I have something to do first. I'll meet you outside the arena gates at eleven o'clock."

Kowalski checked his cell phone clock, then nodded eagerly. Maybe it was time for a little payback.

***

The small studio apartment still smelled vaguely of disinfectant and stale cigarettes, despite the hours it had taken him to clean it yesterday. Fox Walters closed and locked his door, the pretty brunette he was with, giggling and bouncing on the lumpy-looking pullout couch.

"Want a drink?" he asked casually. He knew it was part of the proper procedure, in such circumstances, to play host before playing around.

The girl shook her dark curls. "Uh-uh." She smiled, her dimples deepening alluringly. She was wearing tight

37

jeans, a middy t-shirt, and a pair of flip-flops which she kicked off. She patted the space beside her. "Come here."

Fox raised his eyebrows. This was going to be easier than he'd anticipated. He wondered fleetingly if this girl was really ready to stay with him for the rest of her life. She'd proclaimed her eternal love only moments earlier, swearing to love him forever, if he'd just "do" her. Fox intended to take her up on her offer.

He felt himself becoming aroused at the idea of being with her. She had an excellent figure, a contagious laugh, and a fun-loving attitude. In his young inexperience, she seemed like the perfect woman. He could definitely spend the rest of his time in her embrace.

He moved across the room, and took a place beside her, his hands beginning to shake. All his years of training were about to come to fruition in one orgasmic climax. But, despite those years of specialized lessons, this would be his first time, and he wanted to enjoy every moment. Savor every exquisite move. He was certain he'd be the best lover she'd ever had, knew he could satisfy her as well as himself, and he intended to do so.

He leaned forward, began to kiss her, gently at first, then more passionately. She responded eagerly, sliding her spine down along the back of the couch, taking him with her. She lay supine on the seat, her long legs wrapping around him as he moved over top of her. His hand crept up under her mid-length t-shirt, and found that she wasn't wearing a bra. His breath quickened. He pushed himself up a little, to undo his jeans, and he felt her legs tighten around him.

"Wait," he panted breathlessly, struggling to reach his zipper. "I can't—"

He cut himself off, as her legs squeezed harder, almost hurting him. He thrust his Will at her, but got no reaction, and his eyes widened in shock. She wasn't human. Couldn't be.

"What the--?"

He tried to pull away, found himself trapped in her embracing limbs. Too late, he realized he was caught. He struggled violently, then watched, horrified, as the girl's slender arm slowly stretched into something sharp and sinister. He never even had a chance to cry out, before she ran him through with the pike, and then wrenched it sideways, across his stomach. His guts exploded into agony, erupting from his body, spilling down onto the girl and the couch, and the last thing he saw, was a fountain of his own blood splattering all over her beautiful, deadly smile.

***

Cutter came out onto the small porch of Angel's cabin, his expression sad. She was sitting in one of the Adirondack chairs, gazing at the moon.

She said softly, "I love the moon. I was just thinking about what you said that night in town. About it always connecting us."

He came over and joined her, brushing his hand along her cheek, as he took his place in the other chair. "Angel, don't. Please. I have to go."

"I know. But I don't want you to, Cutter."

"I'll be back as soon as I can, you know that."

"I've just got this feeling that something will happen —Something bad."

"Would you feel better if I took you with me?"

She spun around, finding his pale eyes, and gazed directly into them, looking for confirmation, her own eyes brimming. "You mean it?"

He nodded slowly. "You're the most important person in my life. I want you to meet the others. I want them to meet you."

"Oh, Cutter!" she threw her arms around his neck, hugging him fiercely.

It was only a trip to New York, after all, but even a brief parting would be almost unendurable, moon or no moon.

"Besides, I just remembered, " he spoke into her hair then, almost laughing, and hiding a huge grin. "I can't drive, and I'll need a ride."

She pushed him away, exasperated, and took a playful swing at him. And then he did laugh, and so did she.

Neither of them had any idea what was waiting for them in New York.

39

Chapter 6: Mind Control

"Hey, you!"

The arrogant inflection cut through Angel's exhaustion, and she half stumbled, as she led Cutter into the too-bright truck stop. After two hours on the road, her eyes were bleary, and she felt a bit numb.

Behind her, Cutter caught her as she tripped, then stiffened, turning in the direction of the person who had spoken.

The voice, belonging to a scrawny, beard-shadowed man behind the breakfast counter, continued, as he nodded toward Angel.

"We don't want her kind in here!"

Angel's dark features paled, and she tensed at the man's insult.

"Huh?" Cutter looked at him blankly for a moment. Then it slowly dawned on him, what the owner of the truck stop was getting at.

They didn't have time for this. They'd come into the diner for a quick bite of food, and to use the phone, not to get into a civil rights debate. Cutter's piercing gaze settled on the man wiping the counter, who squirmed under his penetrating glare.

Cutter said, "We only want some coffee and pie, and to use your phone. We don't have any cell service out here."

The thin, stubble-faced man's features registered his displeasure, his eyes shifting away.

"Look at me!" Cutter snapped, drawing the man's attention back to his own face. "The lady will have a coffee and apple pie. I'll have the same."

"--Y--yes. Of course" said the owner in a less-than-enthusiastic tone. But he put away his cloth, and began to get their order.

Cutter nudged Angel toward a booth, but she resisted. "Come on," he urged.

"No." she said, her breath catching. She'd grown up in a small, rural Pennsylvania town, where everyone had known and accepted both her and her family, and she had

41

rarely encountered the obvious bigotry the man displayed. It made her feel small and somehow dirty, yet angry enough to want to confront him.

"Come on!" Cutter insisted.

"But--" she began to protest, even as Cutter moved her to the booth. "That man -- he has no right to--"

"--I know." broke in Cutter, suddenly grinning.

"What are you laughing about?" She demanded, turning her anger on him.

"Can you imagine what he'd be saying, if he knew what *I* am?"

Angel paused, thinking about it, then grinned back, lightening up.

The owner came over with their coffee, a kind of blank look in his eyes. "Pie's coming. Anything else?"

"No," said Cutter. "Where's your phone?"

"In the back."

"Thank you."

The man left, and Angel watched him go, his attitude subdued, his eyes glazed. Something had occurred here, which she couldn't quite put her finger on.

She shrugged it off, said, "So. What are you going to do, when we get to New York?"

"I'm going to see Boomer, if I can."

"Boomer? Who's Boomer?"

"He's the coordinator for this sector. He organizes the settlement of arriving team members, keeps track of who makes it--and who doesn't. He should know something about the missing operatives. Maybe he even knows if there have been any new advances in the grey's tracking methods."

Angel nodded. "You know where to find him?"

But Cutter shook his head. "No. That's why I have to call. I have a number where I can reach him, but that's all."

Their pie arrived at that moment, and neither of them spoke further. They gave their attention to the food, each wrapped in private thought. When they had finished, Cutter rose, excusing himself, and headed for the phones in the back.

* * *

"Cutter?" cried Boomer's delighted voice over the phone line. "We thought your were dead!"

Of course they did. They'd left his injured body beside the wreckage of their ship. Left him for the grey's to find, so that the rest of the team could escape, fully expecting that the greys would find him and finish him. He didn't blame them. He would've done the same, their ultimate mission was that important.

He said, "Well, if I'm dead; I've gone to Heaven."

Immediately understanding, Boomer exclaimed, "You've bonded?"

"Yeah, and I want to be sure we're safe--that the greys have given up searching for me and our team. Any word on that?"

Boomer's voice came back, tense and unhappy.

"Word's out that they're hunting. Hunting hard." he hesitated. "Did you hear about Fox? He survived the crash, but the greys found him. You need to be careful, Cutter. Real careful."

* * *

A fist slammed down hard on the table, making Angel jump. She turned from staring out the window, at the headlights passing on the highway, to find the owner of the truck stop standing over her, his glazed expression replaced by one of clear and undisguised hatred.

"Did your darkie-loving boyfriend desert you?" he asked, meaningfully.

"No." replied Angel cooly, wondering about the change in the man's attitude. Moments ago, he'd seemed dazed, yet, as soon as Cutter had left--

"Uppity little black bitch--" he began, but was suddenly whirled around by his arm, to face Cutter, a gleam of anger in his almost-white eyes.

"Apologize." Cutter spoke softly, and then spun the man back around to face Angel.

He stuttered, the words catching in his throat, but his will was over-ridden by Cutter's, and he stammered, "S-s-sorry, Miss."

Angel's pretty brow puckered in puzzlement. What was going on here? She paid for their food, gathered her purse, and stood, ignoring the apology.

43

"Come on, Cutter."

* * *

Cutter was visibly shaken by news of Fox Walters's murder. When he told Angel, and she attempted to show her sympathy, he nearly exploded.

"You don't understand, Angel! You never will! He was only a kid!" Because of his age, sending Fox had been a hotly debated controversy among the colonization teams. He was brash, young and cocky, but the best member of his team. He and Cutter had trained together, and had become close friends, knowing each other's strengths and weaknesses. And Fox had had few weaknesses. He was the cream of the crop, and they'd been hesitant to send him. His DNA was valuable to them all, too valuable to risk loosing it for the mission. "It shows just how desperate my people have become." Cutter told her. His voice trailed off dismally, but his mind raced ahead. Fox had been exceptional. If the greys had been able to take him out, then something new had been added to their arsenal of weapons. Something totally unexpected. But what was it?

* * *

Jeff led the bearded man up the front steps, and onto the porch, a feeling of disquiet settling over him. Something about the silence surrounding Angel's cabin wasn't quite right. As he stepped up to the front door, he realized what it was:

No dog.

Asti should have been barking up a storm, on the other side of the door, by now.

With this realization, disappointment flooded his awareness. They weren't here.

If Asti wasn't here, then neither was Angel, and if she wasn't around, then neither was that bastard, Cutter Steele.

He turned to the bearded man, who had eventually introduced himself as Ellem Ennopy, a foreigner. That was good---a foreigner! Cutter was certainly in deep. Not only had he come here and made trouble for Jeff, he'd also bilked a British heiress out of millions, before stealing both Ennopy's money and his wife. It was an international scam Cutter was running, and both Jeff and Ennopy were determined to see him stopped.

"They're not here." he told Ennopy, regretfully.

"Good!" said the big man, in his flat monotone, then proceeded to smash in the door.

* * *

Angel held back her questions for as long as she could manage. When her curiosity was finally too much for her to bear, she blurted, "Cutter, just what was going on, back there at the truck stop?" She glanced at him from behind the wheel of her SUV, the on-coming headlights momentarily revealing his chiseled features. In the seat behind her, Asti yawned and settled down.

Cutter's voice came back through the darkness sounding cautious.

"What do you mean?"

"I mean, what was going on? That man behind the counter--one moment he was ready to lynch me, the next he was serving me pie on a pate with extra ice cream, and then-- when you went off to make your phone call-- he was in my face again. I know something was going on. Something to do with you. Now, what was it?"

She downshifted as they approached a tollbooth, and then searched her purse for change, as Cutter considered. He supposed it was about time she learned a little more about him and his people.

"We-- my people and I-- have a kind of-- talent."

"What sort of 'talent'?"

"It's hard to describe. We can force our Will into someone else's mind; force them to do what we want. And, with you humans, it's even easier to do than with one of our own kind."

"So that's what you did back there? You *forced* that guy to serve me?" The idea was almost as insulting as the man's original attitude had been. And then another thought occurred to Angel, one even more revolting, searing itself into her brain. She fought to put it into words, almost choking on them.

"Cutter--is--is that-- Did you do that to *me?*" She remembered now, how it'd been in the beginning, when they'd first met. How he'd so easily convinced her to take

45

him home with her, rather than to the hospital. How she hadn't questioned him about his lack of ID, or about his easy acceptance of her story of encountering the greys. She bit her lip, waiting for his answer. She dropped money into the toll basket, and pulled away, back into the line of traffic, afraid of what he might say, but needing to know.

Of course I did, thought Cutter. *It was to be expected, wasn't it?* How else could he--or other's like him--complete such an important mission?

He said, "Angel, my mission requires--"

"Damn your 'mission', Cutter! I don't want to hear about your damned mission! You brain-washed me!"

"No, it isn't like brain-washing--" he began, but she silenced his defense, down shifting, and pulling onto the off ramp.

"--Just shut up!"

* * *

Cutter couldn't understand Angel's stormy silence, or her anger. According to his culture, he hadn't done anything wrong. It had been only natural for him to use his abilities, hadn't it? Especially to hasten his pair bonding. As he mounted the steps to Boomer's brownstone, Angel cold and silent beside him, he wondered just why she was angry.

Inside, Angel was fuming. How dare he? It was almost like rape! He had purposely pushed his Will into her mind! Forced her to "want" to be with him! Maybe she didn't even care for him, after all. And how could she be sure he wasn't still affecting her brain somehow? She felt like a hostage, not a lover, and the feeling ignited an inner rage which threatened to overwhelm her. She accompanied him up the steps to the brownstone, undecided as to what she wanted to do about the situation. She considered just leaving him there, on the brownstone's steps. She could jump back into her SUV, and drive herself and Asti back to Pennsylvania, and forget all about Cutter Steele, and his damned mission to save his people. His alien people.

Cutter seemed to know what she was thinking. As he raised his hand to push the doorbell, he hesitated, his self-confidence suddenly deserting him. He turned away from her, his odd, pale eyes downcast, and said, softly, "Please, Angel. Don't be angry with me. I only did what I had to do, to make you mine. I--love you."

"But how do I know that I really love you?" She demanded harshly, speaking for the first time since she'd told him to shut up.

He swallowed hard, desperate. "We're pair-bonded, Angel. I no longer have -- 'influence' -over you. Surely you've felt that--haven't you?"

Angel considered. It was true that she seemed to have been feeling more like herself again, lately. And her heart was truly aching over this matter, torn between wanting to love him, and never wanting to forgive him. Perhaps he was telling her the truth. Maybe he could no longer affect her with his Will.

She rubbed at her forehead, confused. "You didn't need telepathy, to make me want you, Cutter." The physical attraction had been there, right from the beginning. The love-- if it was real-- had been there, too. "I just don't know...." He'd tricked her, right from the start.

"Please." he said again, his voice tortured sounding. "We're life-mates. You know what will happen, if you leave me."

Angel stared at his back, a lump forming in her throat, angry with herself now, that she could cause him this torment. He'd die, if she left. Is that what she wanted?

She reached out, and lightly touched his shoulder. He turned, seeing the forgiveness in her eyes, and took her in his arms. "You'll never regret this," he whispered fervently. "I swear you won't."

They stood on the darkened stoop a moment longer, their embrace becoming more passionate, and Angel found herself wondering how she cold possibly have questioned the validity of her love for this man. She tore herself away, smoothing her crushed clothes, and gestured to the doorbell.

Cutter composed himself, and pushed the small, lighted button. They waited a few moments, then tried again.

No one answered the buzzer, arousing Cutter's suspicions. He'd spoken to Boomer less than half an hour ago, arranging this meeting. He tried the door, and found that it was open.

He and Angel exchanged wary looks, and then Cutter shrugged, and went into the brownstone.

They found Boomer alone at the kitchen table, in the back of the house, his throat slashed.

"Oh--*no*--!" whispered Angel, a hand over her mouth to keep herself from screaming.

Although surprised, Cutter was more levelheaded. He began checking for clues to see if he could determine who had killed his friend. There was no weapon in the area, and nothing in the house seemed to have been touched.

"The--greys?" guessed Angel in a tiny voice.

Cutter's lips were tight "Most likely." If they'd found Boomer, then things were worse than he'd thought.

"Why, Cutter?"

He was so preoccupied with his own raging thoughts, that he almost didn't hear Angel's question.

"--What?"

"*Why?* Why are they doing this? You-- never told me why the greys are trying to exterminate your people."

Time for the Truth, he realized. *The whole truth.*

"Because they're afraid of us, Angel. Of what we are-- what we as a species might become. They fear our mental power. They claim that it's corrupted us, that we --abuse-- it."

In light of their previous argument, Angel said nothing. Then, a fleeting thought wormed its way into her consciousness: Might the greys' fears be justified?

"Come on," Cutter said, finally. "Let's get out of here, before the police come."

She followed him dazedly out of the brownstone, the horror of what she'd seen imprinted on her memory. Her life had become a tangled mess, and she was suddenly glad that she hadn't yet told Cutter that she was pregnant.

Chapter 7: On The Run

Stray pulled his jaguar as far as he could off onto the shoulder of the interstate. He heaved an exasperated sigh, and stopped the engine. Just what he needed - a flat tire.

Outside, the rain was coming down in sheets, and it was almost dusk. Other cars whizzed by, their headlights and wipers on, as he pulled the collar of his trench coat up, and got out.

He should've been in New York, by now. The foul weather and heavy traffic had slowed him down, putting him at least an hour behind schedule. He had been working in the New York, Pennsylvania and New Jersey sector for just over a decade now, and should be used to the road conditions. He'd had an appointment in the city around 5pm, but it looked like he wasn't going to make it. Should have left the hotel earlier—

He went carefully around the car and got out his jack and spare, the cold rain dripping down the back of his neck, and murmured an oath under his breath. Of all the days for this to happen! Other cars streaked past, splashing his trench coat and expensive suit. He sighed inwardly, checked his watch, and then began to change the flat.

* * *

"Are you ok?" Cutter asked from his side of the Cherokee. Angel was driving like a lunatic, despite the heavy downpour, and hadn't said anything since they'd left Boomer's, nearly an hour ago.

"Huh?" His words cut into her trance, and Angel almost jumped, startled. She glanced at the speedometer, suddenly aware of the speed at which they were traveling, and then eased off the accelerator a little. She must have been speeding since they left NY; all she'd wanted to do was put as much distance as possible between them and Boomer's brownstone.

She said, "What do we do, now?"

"What do you mean?"

"Cutter, we just left a murder scene!"

The thought practically turned her stomach. She took her eyes off the rain-drenched interstate long enough to look over at him. Behind her, as if sensing her distress, Asti whined.

It was just coming on dusk, but Cutter's hard profile stood out starkly, his pale eyes almost luminous, yet cold.

"Boomer's dead. Nothing we *can* do." he stated unemotionally.

"Well--what if someone saw us? What if we left some kind of evidence that we were there--?"

But Cutter had seen to the details, and he assured her that they'd be all right.

His cold, calculating attitude was unnerving.

"How can you be so--casual--about all of this?" She asked in a small voice.

Cutter gave her a long, searching look. She didn't understand--couldn't possibly know, of course--what his life had always been like. He said, evenly, "Boomer's not the first friend I've lost."

And then it struck her: Fox Walters had been a friend of Cutter's too. How many other friends and acquaintances had Cutter lost in the flight from the greys? How many of his people had they annihilated? He'd told her before, how his whole life had consisted of training and hiding, hoping to avoid their lethal search parties. Had he grown so used to death, that it no longer affected him? The possibility chilled her.

She said, "But doesn't this bother you at all?"

He considered. "I'll tell you what bothers me: Boomer's throat was slashed. The grey's use energy weapons."

The change of topic threw Angel, and she gave her attention to the road before replying. "If--if that's true, and the greys didn't kill Boomer, then who did?"

"That's just it," he said. "It's just like with Fox. No one but the greys had any reason to go after either of them, yet they're both dead--and by unusual means."

For a while Angel drove in silence, thinking. It had been a horrible day. Between finding out about Cutter's strange "talent", and Boomer's murder--and Cutter's cold reaction to it--she was no longer so sure that she wanted to continue their relationship. He had turned her life upside down, and things were getting too intense, too weird, and too scary.

Yet, there was the baby to consider—

On his side of the vehicle, Cutter was quiet, watching her drive, and suspecting the worst. He could tell she was still angry about him using his talents to win her. And she was shook up about Boomer, too. But there was something more, something he was missing. He studied her dark silhouette, wondering what it was.

It began to rain harder, the SUV's headlights revealing the slick surface of the road before them. Up ahead, a car was pulled off on the shoulder, a well-dressed man bent over the car's jack.

Angel shifted her glance to Cutter. "Should we stop?" Ordinarily she wouldn't, but this time she wasn't alone, and she felt compassion for the other traveler, working on changing a flat tire in the rain.

"Huh?" said Cutter, breaking out of his reverie.

"That poor guy's got a flat. Should we stop to help?"

He considered the downpour; knew that whoever the guy was, he'd probably appreciate an extra pair of hands. "Ok."

Angel eased the Cherokee over onto the shoulder of the road, just beyond the stranded Jaguar, and pulled to a stop. She waited as Cutter got out, and ran back to offer his assistance to the other motorist. The steady rain hammered on the roof of the car, and the windows fogged, obstructing her view.

After about 15 minutes, Cutter returned to the SUV, and got in, dripping wet, his pale hair tousled. Asti gave him an inquisitive going-over with his nose.

"How'd you make out?"

"Fine." he said, buckling his seat belt and giving the dog an obligatory pat, as the Jaguar pulled around them, and got back onto the interstate.

"What is it?" probed Angel, also merging back into the line of traffic. She could tell that something had happened.

When Cutter looked up, his face was grim.

51

"That man," he said, "was an FBI agent, on his way to interview Boomer."

* * *

"What?" Angel almost choked, the breath catching in her throat, her heart pounding.

"Look," said Cutter, "he gave me his card." He shoved a business card into her line of vision.

Angel slapped the card away.

"What did you say to him?" she demanded breathlessly.

"I told him what we found at Boomer's--"

"You-you *what?* You told him we were there?" Angel could hardly believe her ears, and glanced from the road to the man beside her in disbelief.

"It's ok," he said calmly. "He's one of us." It had been apparent, the moment their gazes had met. They'd each reached out with their Wills, momentarily locking horns, then simultaneously backed off in realization, and introduced themselves.

"His name's Stray." informed Cutter. "He's been working with the settlement program for the last ten years, and has acquired more information about the murders and disappearances, than anyone. He was on his way to New York to talk to Boomer about Fox."

"You learned all that, while changing a tire?"

Cutter nodded.

"Does this 'Stray' character know about the greys?"

"Of course. Like I said, he's one of us. One of our people."

Angel didn't miss the fact that he was including her, as one of his own race.

"Then--does the FBI know about the greys too?" she persisted.

Cutter shook his head, drops of rain spraying her. "As far as your government knows, he's investigating a string of unrelated 'ordinary' murders, with similar aspects. Possibly copycats." He paused. "Stray had some interesting information for us, though."

Angel gave her attention to the road, pulling onto the exit ramp, and slowing the car, before saying carefully, "Go on."

"The greys have a new weapon, just as I'd thought."

"What kind of weapon?"

"They're using their biomeks."

"Biomeks?" They came to the end of the ramp, and she stopped, waiting for traffic to pass, and then turned to Cutter. "What in the world are biomeks?"

Something the greys had used peacefully for almost a century. But they'd finally done it. They'd converted their biomechanical servants into weapons.

"They're cyborgs." he said flatly. "Biological material with computer brains, and morphing ability. Practically undetectable and indestructible. And now they're programmed to find and eliminate us."

* * *

It was well after dark, when they pulled up in front of Angel's cabin. The events of the day had taken their toll, and they were both exhausted and road-weary as they climbed out of the SUV. Angel dashed through the downpour to the steps of her front porch, and then stopped, her mouth forming a surprised "o".

The front door of her cabin was ajar.

A chill ran down her spine.

"Cutter--?"

He came up behind her, and immediately took-in the situation.

"Stay here." he ordered briskly, then proceeded into the darkened cabin alone.

A few moments later, a light came on inside, and Angel heard him utter a long, low whistle, like any typical human male. He came back to the door and gestured for her to come in.

The scene that greeted her shocked Angel almost as much as finding Boomer dead had. The whole place was in complete disarray. Her home had been totally trashed.

Table drawers had been opened and spilled out, cabinets were emptied, and furniture cushions slashed and tossed aside, their stuffing strewn about.

Behind them in the door way, Asti growled, his hackles raised, and Angel felt another chill run down her back. Could there still be someone else in the cabin?

"What's the matter, boy?" She signaled the dog to

come to her, but he remained in the entry, growling softly.

"He senses something." She said, glancing uneasily around the cabin.

Cutter sniffed at the odor of dampness, which pervaded the interior. "Whoever did this is long gone." he assured her. By the smell of things, the cabin had been left open for a few hours at least. He noticed the flashing light on Angel's land phone.

"You've got messages."

"Huh?" she said. Asti backed out onto the porch, and disappeared, still growling. "Your answering machine. Better check your messages."

"Oh--er--yeah." Angel reluctantly moved farther into her home, still feeling as though they might not be alone in the cabin. She pushed the play button on the machine and, after the usual beep, was surprised at the voice, which spoke.

"Angel? It's Jeff."

So much had happened recently, that it seemed like ages since she'd heard from him. A lifetime.

"Geez, you know how much I hate talking on these things. Sorry you're not in. I'll try again later."

There was a clicking sound as he'd hung up, followed by another beep, and Jeff's voice once more.

"Me again. Pick up if you're there." A moment of silence, another click and beep, and then Jeff's third message:

"OK. I guess I won't get to talk to you, after all. Look, it's just that--I just wanted to tell you--well, I mean, to warn you. A friend of mine shared some news with me, concerning Cutter Steele. He's being investigated by the Feds for fraud. I --uh--well--I just thought you should know." he hesitated, and then continued. "I'll try to get you again later. Or you call me, if you get in. Bye."

There was a final click, then a double click, and the answering machine shut off.

Angel glanced at Cutter, her thoughts awhirl. The FBI again! Is that who had broken into and ransacked her home? It didn't seem likely. She studied Cutter in the light from the ceiling fan, wondering. But why would Jeff lie? Just how much--if anything-- did Jeff know about what was going on?

Cutter caught her staring at him, and grinned, a cocky expression, erasing the tension that had been riding his features since they'd left Boomer's.

The transformation reassured Angel somehow. Whoever--whatever--Cutter Steele was, she loved him.

She said, "How would the FBI even know of your existence?" After all, his name couldn't possibly be in any of their files; she'd made it up herself, only recently.

He shrugged. "They can't. Except for Stray, that is. Your 'friend' must be lying."

She caught the stress he put on the word, and frowned. "But why would Jeff lie about something like that?"

Cutter's grin widened. "Oh, come on, Angel!" Wasn't it obvious? Surely she had to know that Jeff was interested in her, and jealous of their relationship.

But Angel was adamant. "It doesn't make sense, Cutter." Jeff wasn't the type to lie. She thought a moment. "It just doesn't make sense."

"Yes, it does." he corrected her suddenly from across the room.

He'd been standing, holding an object under the light of the ceiling fan, studying it in deep concentration. All at once, he burst into action.

"Come on!" he said. "Find Asti! We can't stay here." He grabbed her roughly by the wrist and began dragging her toward the exit.

"Ouch!" protested Angel. "You're hurting me. What do you mean, 'we can't stay here'? What's gotten into you?"

Cutter turned once, his face pale, a gleam of desperation in his almost-white eyes. He spoke, his voice hard with new knowledge.

"The greys have found me."

* * *

"Where are we going?" demanded Angel, as he ushered her out into the stormy night, back to her Cherokee. Where could they go?

"Just drive!" he commanded, throwing her car door open, and shoving her into the vehicle. He heard Asti

55

barking from somewhere beyond the surrounding trees, and called to him. There was a loud yipe, and a moment later Asti appeared, dripping wet.

"Here, boy!" called Angel, leaning to open the rear passenger door. The yellow lab bounded over, and leaped into the SUV, spraying them with his rain-soaked coat, a happy expression in his brown dog eyes. Cutter slammed the door shut, and then climbed into the front seat next to Angel's.

"Go!" he shouted.

She started the engine, then, spurred by his urgent attitude, whisked them off into the torrential rain and darkness.

* * *

The man known to Jeff as Ellem Ennopy, pulled his gray Nissan into its parking space in front of his motel room, and turned off the engine. He and Jeff had parted company earlier that day, after having searched Angel French's cabin for clues about Cutter Steele. Sure enough, the alien's real identity and presence had been confirmed, and the bearded man had contacted his superiors with the information, before going back to the motel to await further orders.

He knew what those orders were likely to be.

He got out of the car, taking the room's key-card from his pocket, and jogged up the wet stairs to his motel room on the second floor. Passing others as he went, he was oblivious to the stares of those he passed, to their unexpected curiosity at seeing a one-armed man.

He opened the door with the ease and grace of one used to doing everything left-handed, unconcerned with the recent loss of his right appendage. It didn't matter.

If and when the order came to kill Cutter Steele, his left arm would perform the function just fine.

* * *

Cutter held the FBI card in his left hand, as he push-buttoned the phone number with his right, the glow from the gas station's lights filtering through the dirty, wet wind-shield of Angel's SUV and glinting off the cell phone.

When the connection was made, and someone answered, he spoke only two sentences.

"It's Cutter. They've found me."

There was a long pause on the other end, then Stray's voice, sounding tense and worried. "Ok. I've got someplace you can go. Listen carefully."

Chapter 8: Abduction!

Angel crossed the sandy area between the outhouse and the shack, the risen moon lighting her way, a chorus of tree frogs and crickets accompanying her.

She'd just been sick--again. She'd heard all about morning sickness, of course, but what she'd been experiencing recently was constant nausea.

She opened the squeaky screen door, and went back into the hot, one-room shack.

Cutter was sitting at the bare table, examining something beneath the hanging oil lamp, Asti at his feet.

He was so intent, that he hadn't even noticed her absence. Which was good, as far as she was concerned. He still hadn't guessed, didn't suspect, that she was pregnant, and she hadn't told him, either. He said, "Angel, come here. You have *got* to see this."

Asti looked up as she crossed the small room to stand looking over Cutter's shoulder.

"What?" she asked unenthusiastically. They'd driven four hours to get to this shanty shack in the middle of the New Jersey pinelands. It was late, and she was sick and exhausted, not to mention confused over their need to evacuate her peaceful cabin in the mountains. So far, Cutter had only told her that he'd found something that proved that the greys knew where he was.

He held something up to the light for her to see. The thing that had betrayed to him the fact that the greys and their biomek had found him.

"A--*hair?*" she asked in disbelief. That was it? A hair?

But Cutter shook his tousled head, his odd, pale eyes revealing the seriousness of his discovery. "Not like any hair you've ever seen--!" He cursed then, dropping his piece of evidence. It fell towards the floor, landing somewhere on or near the dog's back, and he reached down, automatically making a grab to catch it.

All at once, Asti snarled, teeth bared, and then snapped, with vicious intent. Cutter drew his hand back quickly enough to avoid the bite, surprise written on his features.

"*No!*" commanded Angel harshly, shocked by her pet's behavior. Ordinarily Asti was well mannered, and his nasty action was both unexpected and unwarranted. Her eyes traveled from the dog to Cutter.

"I'm sorry. He's never done that before, " she offered. "Wonder what's gotten into him?" He'd been acting strangely since they'd left her cabin, whining and panting during their hurried trip east, when he normally would have endured the ride in canine silence.

Cutter braved the dog's temper once again, running his hand through the animal's thick fur, looking for the item he'd dropped, inwardly anxious.

This time the dog allowed his exploration, but kept watchful eyes on him, a silent snarl curling is furry lips.

"Gone," exclaimed Cutter, after examining both the dog, and the surrounding floor.

"--How could it be gone?" doubted Angel wearily. "Anyway, it's just a hair, isn't it?"

"That--hair--" he began firmly, "--was made of an artificial substance like nothing on this planet. It's how I was able to tell that a biomek had been in your cabin."

"Just what's so different about it?"

"Well, for one thing, it's *alive.*"

"Alive? Are you kidding? Aren't hairs dead proteins, or something? Like fingernails?"

"Not this hair. Like I said, it's artificial-- yet alive. Capable of independent movement."

The very idea gave Angel the creeps, and she shuddered. Maybe that's what had caused him to drop it-- independent movement.

Asti got up, and began to pace the room, panting.

She said, "Want to go out, boy?" When the dog headed to the back door of the shack, she let him out. "Don't get lost." she called after him, as he disappeared into the surrounding scrub pines. She took a deep breath of the salty night air, and then turned back to Cutter, closing the door. "What are you doing?" He was on the bare tile floor, running his hands over the gritty surface, searching.

"I've got to find that hair," he said.

"Why?"

He paused, sighing deeply. "I don't know, maybe I'm wrong, maybe it's too small to matter--"

"What are you talking about?"

"The biomek that hair belongs to just might be able to trace it. Track it down. Use it as a homing device. " He got up off the floor, rubbing absently at his knees. "Unless it's too small---" his voice trailed off uncertainly, then came back stronger. "Maybe Stray will know for sure."

"When's he getting here?"

"By morning, at the latest." Stray had been in New York, when Cutter had called him, and had had some business to wrap up, before he could meet them at the place to which he'd directed them, this lonely shack in the middle of nowhere.

"Well, we can't find that hair in this light," said Angel. "Might as well go to bed, and wait till daylight. Come on, help me with the fold-out---"

Cutter nodded. "OK," he agreed, and began to help her open the couch.

Outside, Asti began to howl.

* * *

The intensity of a brilliant light awakened Cutter around four AM. Since there was no electricity in the off-grid shack, he woke confused, squinting his eyes, and wondering where the light was coming from. It seemed to emanate from all around him, from all four windows and both doors, flooding into the building with laser-like sharpness.

He tried to glance round, suddenly aware that he couldn't move, and his heart lurched. Someone appeared in the corner of the room, advancing toward the pull-out couch, moving out of the shadows and into the intense glare. The hairs stood up on the back of Cutter's neck, as he recognized the familiar form of a grey, its large, black oval eyes unblinking, unreadable. Another one appeared, then another.

Cutter struggled against the energy field that held him in place, his pulse racing. They'd come for him! But how had they located him? Surely that hair from the biomek had been too small to--

The first grey took a device from its wrist sheath, and pointed it toward the couch. What was it doing? There was an odd dampening of sound, and Cutter felt the energy field ripple against his skin. Beside him, Angle stirred, coming awake.

He saw her momentary confusion abruptly change to terror as she spied the small grey beings that now surrounded the couch. Her dark eyes widened; flew to Cutter's face.

"Cutter?" she cried, clutching the blanket which covered them to her throat.

How could she speak aloud? How could she move? Cutter remained paralyzed, unable to do either, his mind racing along with his heart, while his body remained stationery, captive in the energy field.

The first grey gestured with his device, and Angel's body rose from the couch, the blanket trailing in her frightened grasp, uncovering her companion. She rose in a horizontal position, and then floated toward the grey that held the device.

No! Cutter screamed inwardly. They were taking Angel! The shack's front door was open, and Angel moved towards it, toward whatever lay beyond it, beyond the blinding light.

She squirmed, trying to look back at Cutter caught in her floating bubble of energy. "Cutter?"

The fear in her voice knifed into Cutter Steel's heart, and he struggled harder against the encasing energy field, feeling the pressure increase as he fought it, knowing it was useless.

Even as Angel moved through the door, his speeding thoughts continued to wonder how they'd been found. His gaze flitted wildly about the room, seeking some means of escape, then lit on Asti, lying calmly by the back door, despite the alien strangers in the shack.

Asti hadn't been let back in, last night.

A chill ran down Cutter's spine, despite the warmth of the energy envelope. Asti--? Could the *dog* have led the greys here?

Angel disappeared out the door, partially blocking the encroaching light. Another moment, and she'd be gone, a prisoner of the grey aliens.

Cutter stopped fighting the surrounding force field; felt its grip loosen a little. Maybe there was a way out of this, yet. He calmed his breathing, forced his muscles to relax, testing. Again, he felt a lessening in the field's power. With a Herculean effort, he pushed his Will against the energy field, and felt it give. Another shove, and it released him. He was immediately up and moving toward the door through which Angel had just disappeared. He was almost there, when a large, one-armed figure suddenly blocked the exit.

* * *

Asti jumped to his feet, brushed past Cutter, to the man in the doorway.

Ellem Ennopy grinned at the canine, extending the stump of his right arm.

The dog leaped, teeth exposed, to grip the stump fiercely. And the furry dog-body suddenly morphed, condensing and melting into the shape of an arm. A strong, muscular arm that just as suddenly dealt Cutter a harsh blow, sending him reeling.

He hit the sandy floor, stunned, and saw the big man's arm change again, as he took a large stride toward Cutter. The appendage became a weapon, a blade, moving in a downward arc, bent on decapitation.

There was little Cutter could do, still stunned by the mighty blow. He rolled to avoid the blade, his reflexes slower than normal. The blade fell, and he felt the swift breeze of its passage, rolled once more. The biomek recovered from the miss, and came at him again. Its left arm stretched, elongated, grabbed Cutter's ankle in a vise-like grip. The blade rose again, this time as if in slow motion, reflecting the light from the doorway and windows. At the top of it's arc, it hesitated, then--with an explosive sound-- it all at once burst into millions of glittering pieces, which rained down onto the floor of the shack, bouncing and rolling in all different directions.

Cutter shook himself in disbelief. There, in the doorway, stood Stray, a gun in his hand.

"Come on!" Stray shouted. "It's not deactivated! It won't stay disintegrated for long, we've got to get out of here!"

Cutter pulled himself to his feet, shaking off his shock, and-- without even a word of thanks-- pushed past Stray, out into the brightly lit night.

Beyond the shack's clearing, a stand of pines almost hid the source of the intense light. Barefoot, and dressed only in a pair of boxer shorts, Cutter dove into the stand of brush-needled pines, his only thought, to save Angel.

* * *

He came out of the scrub, and into a burned-out area. At the center of a blackened circle of parched ground, sat the grey's ship. It was an ugly lump of metallic grey, the subject of Cutter's childhood nightmares.

The entry portal was open, flooding the surroundings with brilliant light. In front of the portal, silhouetted by the glare, was a group of greys, the horizontal shape of Angel floating in their midst.

As he burst out of the tree line, they were just guiding the energy field containing Angel into the ship.

"No!" whispered Cutter, horrified, at a dead run.

Behind him, Stray arrived, breathing hard.

Not sure if the greys were aware of his presence, and without thought to his own safety, Cutter emerged into the clearing at an all out run. He had to stop them! He had to get Angel back!

The greys were just disappearing into their squat ship, the portal already closing. Cutter covered the charred sandy ground, desperation hot on his heels, and arrived just as the entry narrowed to an opening the size of his thigh's width.

He screamed as he attempted, with all of his strength, to keep the aperture from closing further, tried to force himself through the narrowing space.

"Angel!"

But his only answer was an explosion of intense pain, as a hot bolt of blue radiance shot through the opening. Then the portal sealed, and Angel was gone.

Chapter 9: Gravid

Jeff Kowalski watched Ellem Ennopy enter the small, seedy motel room. The large man's expensive suit was in ruins, hanging from his broad shoulders in tatters, exposing his well-formed muscular arms.

"What happened to you?"

Ennopy shrugged the question off, shedding his shredded apparel as he crossed to the bathroom to wash up.

"Where's Steele?" demanded Jeff. Ennopy was supposed to have brought the gold-digging interloper back with him.

Ennopy stopped, then turned and said flatly, "Gone." He knew exactly where Steele was, but wasn't about to inform the impatient human.

"What do you mean? I thought you were tracking them with some kind of homing device. How could you loose them?"

"Not 'them'. Him. The woman's with my superiors."

Jeff considered, breathing the stale cigarette smell of the rented room. So Ennopy had lost Steele, but Angel was in custody. What would Ennopy's superiors want with Angel? He asked.

"She's being questioned about Cutter Steele, of course. It's no concern of yours."

Questioned. Interrogated? All kinds of movie scenes flashed through Jeff's over imaginative mind. "If they hurt her--"

"They won't," cut in the big man evenly. "So just forget about her. She's Steel's woman anyway." He almost succeeded in sneering.

"Not if I have anything to say about it--"

"--She's carrying his child." This time Ennopy did sneer.

Kowalski stuttered and choked, his face reddening in rage.

"Wha--?"

Angel was pregnant? That bastard had--!

Ennopy ignored the other man's reaction,

disappearing into the bathroom, his words muffled by the shutting of the door.

"Forget her."

* * *

"Forget about Angel, for now." Advised Stray in a level voice. "Those ships are practically impregnable, so forget about trying to attack them. Just concentrate on healing."

"You know I can't do that." Cutter's jaw was set, a stubborn look in his pale eyes.

Stray finished bandaging the other's burned arm, then turned away with a morose sigh. Cutter was right. Stray knew as well as he did, what Angel's absence meant, both mentally and physically to Cutter. If they didn't have Angel back in about two weeks, Cutter would begin to die.

Cutter stared out the window, at the cottage next door, absently rubbing his injured arm, where the blue ray of energy had torn through his flesh. The wound had cauterized immediately, but the burned gash it had left was still in danger of infection, and intensely painful.

The sound of the ocean was a backdrop for the intermittent cries of laughing gulls, and the scent of salt air blew in through the room's open windows. They were in a small, rented bungalow, one block from the beach, in North Wildwood, New Jersey, in the middle of tourist season. It would be hard for the greys or their biomecks to spot them here, but they still weren't safe.

Cutter frowned grimly, thinking of Angel. He knew the kind of things the greys did to humans. The--*tests*. He and Stray were still in danger, but Angel was actually in the hands of the enemy. The very idea sent adrenalin coursing through his veins. His anxiety wasn't what Stray thought, however. There was no concern, yet, for himself and the danger Angel's absence would cause to his health. He was worried only for her. What were the greys doing to her? What unspeakable experiments would they perform on his wife?

He stood and began to pace, the pain of his injured arm overridden by his tormented concern for his mate.

Aloud, he said, "If the greys realize that Angel's sick--"

65

"What?" Stray pulled himself out of his own interrupted thoughts, at Cutter's words.

"Angel's been sick a lot, lately. They greys will want to do all kinds of tests--" The thought was almost too much to bear.

Alerted, Stray's features pulled into a frown. "You never said anything. What's wrong with her?"

Cutter continued to pace, shrugging. "I don't know much about human health. I never saw any of our people get sick every morning, like she does. She hasn't mentioned the cause, so perhaps it's not serious. I don't know. I just want her back."

The anguish in his voice prevented Stray from speaking at once. He became quiet. Too quiet. When he finally spoke, his words were carefully chosen. "You said she's been sick every morning?"

Cutter nodded wordlessly.

"Dizziness?" questioned the other tightly.

"Once or twice."

Stray gulped. He'd been here long enough to know the symptoms. "We've got to find a way to get her back as soon as possible, Cutter. She could be pregnant."

Pregnant.

The word fueled a desperation Cutter had never known, in all the years he'd been running from the greys. Pregnant. With Child. *His* child! If Stray was right, and he'd succeeded in his mission, a new generation of their people was already in gestation. A generation that had to be protected at all costs.

His pale eyes shot to Stray, their burning gaze revealing Cutter's renewed determination. "I don't care what it takes, you've got to help me get her back!"

* * *

The sound of repetitive screaming brought Angel to full consciousness. She had been drifting somewhere in a state of drowsy unreality, in which time had been meaningless. The screaming had become an annoyance that had finally broken through her befuddled condition, returning her to full awareness.

She jumped, gasping, her eyes wide, just as the screaming stopped.

Where was she?

She gazed around at the unfamiliar surroundings, which smelled somehow antiseptic. She was in a small, oval chamber, with an arched ceiling. Light emanated from the walls, ceiling, and floors, in a dim level that strained her eyes. Above her, suspended from the curved ceiling, was a metallic contraption, full of needle-like projections that filled her with terror. She turned her head away, suddenly realizing that she was lying on a table of some sort, restrained by a cushion of invisible pressure.

She struggled against the energy field but, quickly tired by the effort, desisted. Her eyes again traveled over the confines of the softly lit area, searching for an exit, but to no avail. There was nothing to break the monotonous curve of wall and arched ceiling. No doors, no portals. It was like being inside a huge egg. How had she gotten *in* here?

She felt like she was buried alive, and the thought panicked her. She began to hyperventilate, the quiet, seamless chamber bringing on a bout of claustrophobia, and she was all at once aware that it had been her own screams that had brought her back to her senses. She was alone and trapped, held in restraint, in this tomb-like cell, with no entry or exit. Alone and beginning to choke on the gradually depleted air supply.

And then, out of nowhere, the first grey materialized.

* * *

A yellow full moon hung over the crashing surf, beyond the long boardwalk. It reflected off the Atlantic's waves, joined by the dazzle of lights from the arcade on the pier above the sand. The cry of gulls mingled with the musical sounds of the amusements and hawkers and crowds of tourists mobbing the boards.

A tramcar approached, making its slow way along the crowded wooden walkway, its mechanical recording warning the pedestrians. "Watch the tram car, please . . . watch the tram car, please..."

A man stepped off the moving tram, and worked his way through the knot of people watching the sky ride, over to one of the wayside benches. He was slightly paunchy, and dressed in shirt and shorts and sandals, and looked like any of the other middle-aged people who were enjoying the late summer evening.

He addressed the two men sitting on the bench, facing the ocean. "Nice night for a walk."

Stray and Cutter stood in unison, turning to the newcomer.

Stray said, "Then let's walk."

* * *

The carnival atmosphere and crowds of people provided the privacy and cover they required for their conversation.

The newcomer was Ace Covington, an operative out of Burlington, New Jersey. He was balding and paunchy, with comfortable dark features that belied his quick, analytical mind, and he knew more about the grey's technology than anyone else earth-side.

As the three men strolled the boards, they spoke easily, unconcerned by the multitudes around them.

Ace said, "I hear you want to penetrate one of their ships."

Cutter said firmly, "We *have* to."

"What is it, some kind of rescue operation?" asked the other casually.

"Is it possible?" questioned Stray. Of the three of them, he was the only one who looked out of place in their beach attire, seeming almost naked without his usual suit and tie.

At first, Ace didn't answer. When he finally spoke, his words were slow and cautious. "You're asking a lot. Do you know which ship, and where it is now?"

"We just want to know if it's even possible!" spat Cutter, his pale eyes flashing, his voice louder than necessary.

"Shhh!" cautioned Stray, placing a hand on his friend's arm.

Ace's mouth pulled into a grim smile. "It's a woman, isn't it? Your pair bond?"

Stray gave him a level gaze, and said quietly, "She may be pregnant."

Covington almost tripped. They all knew the importance of such a possibility. He said, "How far along is she?"

"What difference does that make?" demanded Cutter harshly.

"Listen, my friend," said Ace seriously. "If she's been gone more than a day or two, she's probably no longer with child."

"What do you mean?" asked Stray.

"Come on! You've been here long enough to know." Ace's voice had a hard edge. "The grey's harvest any mixed-species pregnancies they discover--"

Despite his best effort, a groan escaped Cutter's throat, his dark features paled.

"Then time is of the essence," stated Stray. "*Is* it possible to penetrate one of their ships?"

Covington opened his mouth to answer, but was cut short by a cry from Cutter, who suddenly moved off in a different direction.

"Angel?"

"Cutter, that can't possibly be--" began Stray, following in the other's footsteps.

Up by the end of the boardwalk, just outside a knot of people, stood a slim, dark woman. She turned, as Cutter called. Her face wore a dazed expression, her eyes glazed, but a small light of recognition crept into them, when she saw the man approaching her. He reached for her.

She said softly, "Cutter?" Then she collapsed into his arms.

* * *

Cutter came out of the bungalow, to stand over Stray and Ace, who were sitting on the concrete stoop, watching the tourists passing by on their ways to and from the boardwalk. Beyond them and the houses across the street, the lights of a giant Ferris wheel twinkled against the darkening sky.

"How is she?" asked Stray.

Cutter heaved a sigh, his features serious. "Dazed and confused. She's asleep now." She hadn't spoken, other than to ask where she was, and how she'd gotten

69

there. She appeared to be numb with shock, mentally traumatized, but there were no signs that she'd been ill-treated physically.

Ace said, "Let her sleep an hour or two, but then we've got to move."

"Why? She's been through enough--"

Ace rubbed a hand across his balding scalp. As he knew from previous experience in his time earth-side, it was always hard dealing with the friends and loved ones of those who'd been abducted. He said, "Because she's been implanted. You know that, Cutter. You can't tell me you didn't check."

Cutter's lips drew into a thin, hard line. "Yes, I checked." And Angel did have the telltale mark, just above her left elbow, of an implanted tracking device.

"Then you know you've got to keep moving."

"She's weak--"

"She'll manage."

"She's also still pregnant." He'd checked that, too. His Will had sensed it, the other little life within her. Why hadn't she told him? She knew his mission, and the importance of its success. Why had she kept the information to herself?

Covington nodded. Angel was still pregnant. Luckily for her, she was still in her first trimester, too early for the greys to remove the embryo for their certain experimental purposes. He said, "All the more reason to keep moving. They'll want to take that embryo, once it reaches the right--"

"You're talking about my *child*," exploded Cutter. All his life had been geared for this possibility, and his paternal emotions and instincts were overwhelming his logic.

Stray spoke up, his voice quiet but firm. "Cutter. They dropped Angel here, on the boardwalk. That means they know where you are. Precisely. They're watching every move you make. Ace is right. You and Angel have got to run. They'll track you, so you've got to keep ahead of them, but you've got to go."

Cutter didn't say anything. He couldn't because he knew that both Ace and Stray were right.

Chapter 10: A Question of Trust

The grey spoke to her without speaking. It put pictures into her head using some kind of technical device. Disturbing pictures. Scenes of horror and violence of such magnitude it was unthinkable. She understood these scenes, without the need of language, and they terrified her as much as the grey that was approaching her did--

Angel woke with a start, the afterimage of those terrible scenes still imprinted on her mind, her heart hammering. The dream had been just like what had happened in real life, when she'd been abducted by the greys.

Cutter sat on the ground beside her, his pale eyes full of concern. "Are you alright?"

She sat up, looking around. It was almost dark, and she was lying on her sleeping bag, between a campfire and her SUV. Stray was adding wood to the fire, and the newcomer, the man named Ace who had finally re-joined them when they'd arrived here, was unpacking some camping gear. She yawned, remembering where they were, and gave Cutter a wary look.

"I'm fine." But the scenes that had been playing in her mind were sharp on her memory, blotting out the surrounding outline of dark trees with images of enslavement and genocide. She shuddered.

For the past two months they had been moving south, from campground to campground, and had ended up in the central Florida woods, hoping to elude the greys and their biomeks, but she hadn't outrun the fear of them, and the confining trees and darkening sky felt ominous.

Cutter was looking at her with an odd expression she couldn't define. "What?" she asked.

He indicated their two companions, and shook his head slightly. "Later." He said.

Angel found herself getting annoyed. Tired and annoyed. Tired of all of the running, and annoyed with the games of secrecy Cutter had been playing.

Stray heard their exchange from his place by the

fire. He knew that right now, more than anything, Cutter would need to speak with his woman in private. They hadn't had much privacy in the past eight weeks; it was about time they talked. He nudged Ace, said, "Come on. Help me get some more fire wood."

"We won't need—" began the other, and then stopped. He eyed Stray, then the couple, then Stray. "Oh, uh-- yeah. Good idea." He put down the camping equipment, and followed Stray into the nearby trees.

When they had gone, Angel gave Cutter a demanding look. "Well?" He was still wearing that intense expression which she couldn't identify.

He blew out a breath, and said, "Why haven't you told me you're carrying our baby?" Although she was already five months pregnant, she was hardly showing, and had never yet spoken of her condition to Cutter.

Angel stared into the campfire, reluctant to put into words the way she'd been feeling. After a long moment, she turned back to him and said, "Why didn't you tell me that your people once enslaved the greys?"

Cutter looked stunned, then angry. "Where did you hear that particular item of propaganda?"

Angel stiffened, becoming angry herself. "Propaganda? Are you going to sit there and tell me it's not true?" Isn't that what the greys had shown her, when they'd filled her head with those scenes of violence?

Cutter hesitated. "What if it was? What difference would it make?"

"A hell of a lot of difference! Cutter—how can I trust you, if you're not being straight with me?"

"I'm being straight with you—"

"Not about the greys." She countered. "And that's why I didn't tell you about the baby. I haven't felt like you're being totally honest with me." She knew what having a baby would mean to him and his people, but what if his race actually had enslaved the greys? What if they were even now abusing their telepathic talents to try to enslave humans as well?

Cutter closed his eyes, his lips a thin line, his breathing slow and heavy as though he was just barely controlling himself. All at once he opened his eyes and

73

stood up, yanked opened the door of the SUV, and began to rummage around in its interior. He straightened; his fist full of money, slammed the door, and began to walk away.

"Where are you going?" demanded Angel.

"We need some food." He said shortly, and began walking toward the path to the campground's small grocery store.

"Cutter—" Angel began.

"—Stray and Ace'll be back. You'll be fine." He answered tightly, and stalked off down the darkened path through the woods.

* * *

The silver Nissan cruised slowly up the dirt road, through the gathering darkness. With his cybernetic brain, Ellem Ennopy concentrated on both his driving, and the clear signal being given off by the woman's tracking implant.

The signal had brought him to this particular recreational park, a campground in the Florida tourist area, and a certain excitement flooded his biomek nervous system at the thought that he was nearing his quarry. His superiors wanted to re-attain the woman. Her pregnancy was advancing, and soon it would be time for them to harvest her fetus, a fetus they greatly desired. One that contained the DNA of Cutter Steele, her pair-bonded mate.

Thoughts of Steele quickened Ennopy's heartbeat. Cutter Steele was one of his Enemy's ultimate successes in their genetic program, a person who carried the traits, drives and abilities, which might enable the Enemy to ultimately repopulate their race on this planet. Now that they were aware of Steele's importance to his people's plans, Ennopy's superiors wanted Cutter Steele dead, and his in-utero child in their laboratories.

Crickets sounded their chirping chorus as the silver Nissan passed down the dirt road leading to the campground's registration office and recreation hall, but Ennopy ignored the noise, concentrating on the signal of the tracking device. He pulled the car into the parking space farthest away from the buildings, and shut off the engine, waiting.

Darkness had fallen, but the full moon was high, and he decided to delay carrying out his mission until after the moon had again set. Light poured from the rec hall, spilling onto the grass in front of Ennopy's car, and music mingled with the laughter of both the people inside, and those hanging around by the soda machine in front. Across the rutted parking lot, a small grocery store advertised firewood for sale, as well as ice and bug spray. In his rear view mirror, movement caught Ennopy's eye as someone came out of the store.

All of his cyborg senses reacted, when he realized it was Cutter Steele.

Now he was caught between two mission parameters: killing Steele, or retrieving the woman. He quickly calculated. The parking lot was far too crowed to hit Steele here. The woman was likely to be alone in the wooded campsites, and vulnerable. He got out of the car, and followed a sign pointing the way to the latrines.

The path was tree lined and dark. He left the noise of the rec hall behind, his cybernetic eyes guiding him on the lonely trail, and along the way, he morphed into a different form.

* * *

Ace Covington burst out of the woods, his eyes large, and his voice urgent.

"Come on, we've got to get out of here!"

Stray looked up from his conversation with Angel, an alarm going off in his brain. Covington was not the type to be easily excited. "What's up?"

"A biomek! Up at the office—" he'd come out of the latrine and spotted Ennopy, recognizing the specific form of a mek, then taken a short cut back to the camp site. He didn't have to say more.

Stray threw dirt on the fire and grabbed Angel by the wrist. "Into the jeep! We're moving out."

"What about Cutter--?" began Angel. He'd been gone a long time, and hadn't come back yet.

"He'll understand. We'll get word to him later."

"I'm not leaving without him—" she argued, but Stray cut her off.

"—His orders were to protect you. We're leaving."

75

"The greys'll only track me—"

"I've got an idea about that," said Covington, throwing the sleeping bags, unrolled, into the back of the Cherokee. The keys were already in the ignition.

Stray grabbed Angel, pushing her toward the car. "Don't argue! Think of your baby!"

With a backward glance at the wooded path Cutter had taken, Angel got into the SUV.

A moment later, they were roaring out of the campground.

* * *

When Cutter came out of the general store, it was already dark. The moon was up, and the night breeze carried a hint of pine. He crossed the parking lot, then stood outside of the rec hall, listening to the merriment inside. He put the groceries he was carrying down on the park bench in front of the rec hall's large window, and sat down sideways, so he could watch the game of ping-pong taking place inside. The sight of people laughing and enjoying their evening made him feel lonely and depressed after the words he'd had with Angel. The fact that she didn't want to trust him tore him apart. He'd never been in love before, he hadn't had time, and when he'd fallen in love with Angel, he'd fallen hard. He'd trusted her with his very life, so it was an agony to think that perhaps she didn't feel the same way about him. He sat on the bench, miserably watching the other campers having fun, and thought again about the American Dream. The dream that had become his goal: to find a mate and a home, and live Happily Ever After. Unfortunately that dream didn't include a life on the run from the greys.

He watched the ping-pong game for a while longer, and then decided to return to the campsite. Perhaps he could convince Angel to trust him after all. He hadn't told her the entire truth about his people's past, and now realized that that had been a mistake. She should have heard it from him. It occurred to him now that, being of African descent; she would naturally be more sensitive to the subject of slavery. He should have given her more information about his race's history. Now it might be too late. She'd learned something from her contact with the greys, and whatever it was, it might be too damaging to repair.

He got up from the park bench, grabbed the grocery bag, and started back down the path toward their campsite, his thoughts anguished. The trail was rough with tree roots, and he picked his way along in the darkness, all of his thoughts centered on Angel. He must make her understand!

He was about half way back to their camp site, when someone came up the path from the opposite direction, and he heard a familiar voice call, "Cutter?"

"Angel?" his heart leaped at the sound of her voice. He'd been gone overly long; perhaps she loved him enough to have come looking for him. He strode forward quickly, eager to speak with her, then suddenly stopped in his tracks.

The voice and form were Angel's, but the movement was not.

Something about the swing of her gait alerted him. He was now barely a pace from the darkened figure. It was not Angel. He threw the bag of groceries at the facsimile, and half turned, ready to run.

Angel extended her arm, as it morphed into a long sharp pike, and speared him just below the collarbone. Her other arm came up and swung a backhand at his head, knocking him almost senseless, and he fell backward to the ground, impaled.

She spoke in a deep, masculine growl. "Where's the woman?" She held out something before Cutter's face. Something small and metallic.

Cutter's vision swam, but he recognized the object. A tracking device. Angel's implant! His thoughts raced. The biomek hadn't found Angel; she was gone! And somehow her tracking implant had been removed.

The biomek morphed its façade into a hideous beast, at the same time twisting the pike in Cutter's shoulder. He screamed, and the biomek leaned closer, regarding him with dispassionate eyes. "Where is the woman?" it repeated.

"I—don't know—" gasped Cutter. If Angel was gone, if she'd deserted him, perhaps she didn't love him after all, and he would be better off dead. He couldn't live without her, that much he knew. He said, "Go ahead. Kill me."

"You *will* die," responded Ennopy.

And then everything in Cutter's world went black.

Chapter 11: Familiar Contempt

"You've got to be kidding me."

The words were out of my mouth before I knew I had said them. I cursed myself for a fool; I should have kept my damned mouth shut. I was so caught up in the marvelous story I was recording that, for the moment, I had forgotten that I was a reporter. I was, almost literally, entranced by the old man - Cutter, I amended mentally - and his story. His baritone voice, rough and cracking the way old men's voices do, was remarkably well suited towards storytelling.

The dim light from the lantern nearby reflected in his eyes as he glared over at me. Again, I felt trapped by his gaze. If his story were true, I knew those eyes to be alien eyes with the ability to mentally compel me.

"I never," Cutter said distastefully, "kid about Angel."

Shit. He took it personally. Screw the assignment, I thought. I just want to hear the rest of this story.

"Cutter, I'm ---" I stopped when his head turned on whip-like tendons and I was struck by the full force of both of his eyes.

"Never," he hissed, "call me 'Cutter' again."

"But I-," I began.

"I stopped using that name," he interrupted me, "when I lost the only thing worth living, or dying, for."

I felt like a chastised nine-year-old who had called his mother by her given name. I was devastated. I dimly realized that I was so engrossed in the story that I felt an intimacy with the old man that simply wasn't there. I had to somehow do some serious damage control and get him to continue with the story.

"What, then," I tried to sound accommodating and formal, "shall I call you?"

Those laser-beam eyes of his turned away and looked again at the moon, now much higher in the sky than before. I followed his gaze unconsciously, remembering the beginning of our conversation.

"You said your happiest moments were when you

shared the moon together, right?"

"You know damned well I said that," snapped the old man crankily. "You have that infernal device hooked into your skull that's recording everything I say. Makes you look like a red-eyed demon, it does." He glanced over at me, "You can call me Al." He chuckled at his stale wit, "Short for Alien."

I groaned appropriately at the pun, but was pleased that his sense of humor had returned. The story was what was important here. If I were lucky, I might be able to hear the rest of it tonight. The thought of trudging back out to this desolate swamp to finish the interview made me shudder.

"Disbelief." Al stated simply.

"What?" I asked absently as I checked the remaining time on my recorder.

"Look at me when I talk to you boy. You want the story; you'd better record everything. Even these little interludes of ours." Dutifully, I turned the recorder back on.

"What about my tale caused you to express disbelief?"

"The biomeks," I answered. "Their ability to shape shift is - fantastic - to put it mildly. You have them assuming the form a family pet so perfectly that no one can tell the difference. Now you have one shifting from a man to a woman." I used my hands for comparison, "It's impossible. Where does all the extra mass go?"

"Ahh!" Al crowed gleefully, "You do have a brain after all."

I was irritated at how grateful I felt at the oblique compliment. How I had allowed myself to get into a position where his approval meant something to me was a mystery.

Oblivious to my internal aggravation, Al continued, "That, my young friend, is the key to the ultimate destruction of all the biomeks on Earth."

I settled back down, recognizing the resumption of the tale.

Chapter 12: Captive Thoughts

The sound of constant traffic kept Angel awake. That, and the unfamiliar couch on which she was lying. She found herself longing for her own bed, in her own cabin in the mountains.

Two weeks had passed since she'd left the Florida campground with Ace and Stray. Being the tech wizard that he was, Ace had quickly removed the tracking device from her arm, while Stray drove. He'd tossed it into a campfire as they'd passed, knowing that the warmth would prevent the device from immediately signaling to the grey's that it'd been removed, and thereby giving the trio a chance for escape.

They'd headed north again, taking turns driving, sometimes traveling I95, other times sticking to the back roads, always moving. When they reached Georgia, Stray had parted company with Ace and Angel, to go back and look for Cutter. He'd had his official ID, and would have no trouble contacting his associates in the government for help. Ace and Angel had continued north, eventually returning to Pennsylvania, where Covington knew some people in Philadelphia. He took Angel to a safe house, where he left her with friends, and returned to his job at a software company, promising to keep in touch and let her know when Stray or Cutter contacted him through their network.

So, here she was, almost six months pregnant, and alone among strangers. She tossed fitfully on the strange sofa in the little row house, listening to the continuous traffic, and wanting nothing more than to be home with Cutter beside her. As she lay there in the darkness, she felt movement inside of her, and wondered for the millionth time about the baby growing in her womb. Half human, and half—alien. Her baby. Cutter's baby.

Then the thought that had been plaguing her for the last two weeks, struck her again, of how Stray had convinced her to leave the campground by insisting that she think of her baby first. How had he known that she was pregnant? She'd only just told Cutter! How had they figured it out? She was just barely showing, and hadn't told either of the men about her constant sickness, yet they'd known.

She grew tired of tossing around on the couch, and got up, to look out the window. She was in the small living room of a tiny row house in the Italian section of Philly, near Delaware Avenue, a block from the waterfront. The neighborhood was old and tired looking, with rows of attached brick homes, and streets so narrow a person could sit indoors and speak to someone in the house across the street. One block over, Delaware Avenue, the old warehouse district had been converted to stylish piers, with shops and gymnasiums and restaurants that stayed open all night, and the flow of traffic and sounds of ships arriving at docks was a background lull that never ceased. The street beyond the window was lit by streetlights, and the glow filtered through the lace curtains, bathing Angel in a light that seemed almost alien to her backwoods past.

She almost laughed at that idea, considering her circumstances, running from real aliens, and at the same time, carrying one in her belly. She turned away from the window, deciding she was hungry, and headed for the kitchen. She crossed quietly through the small living room, through the dining room, and into the tiny kitchen. As she opened the refrigerator, she heard the stairs squeak, and turned to find the owner of the house, a woman in her mid fifties, entering the room.

"Couldn't sleep?" she asked Angel. She was a petite woman named Toni, with salt and pepper hair, dark complexion and a ready smile.

Angel shook her head, said, "I'm famished."

Toni grinned. "When are you due?" Ace had brought the young woman here, asking Toni to give her a place to stay, no questions asked, and she'd agreed. She was aware of Ace's connections with what she called the Resistance, aware of the existence of the greys, and knew that this woman must be avoiding them, but she didn't need to ask why.

Angel gave Toni a blank look. In all the time that she'd known about her pregnancy, she hadn't been to a doctor, had no idea of her exact due date. Suddenly, she felt like crying. This wasn't the way it was supposed to be! All the running, all the hiding, all the fear.

Toni patted her hand. "Never mind, hon." She said, sympathetically. "I'm here for you."

* * *

Ellem Ennopy stood in the doorway, regarding his prisoner, and considering his options.

Cutter Steele sat slumped forward, unconscious; his hands cuffed behind him to the chair back, his eyes blindfolded. For the past two weeks, Ennopy had allowed Jeff Kowalski to torture Steele in an effort to obtain the information that the greys wanted, but to no avail. Cutter hadn't talked. Ennopy hadn't expected him to. Steele was trained as a soldier, and was one of the toughest people his race had to offer. But Ennopy had still allowed Kowalski his fun. He found it extremely interesting that Kowalski had seemed to enjoy hurting the blond man, becoming angry when he was ordered not to go too far. But the woman was gone, and they needed to find her, and Ennopy knew that his only means of accomplishing that task was through Steele. Eventually, he'd sent Kowalski away, and now stood appraising the possibilities and estimating his chances for success.

He knew that in just a few days, Steele would begin to feel his separation from the woman as a physical sensation that, if left untreated by reunion, would become a new kind of torture, one that could, and would, kill. An urgent struggle for life that would lead Cutter to hunt for Angel himself.

He decided to wait it out.

* * *

Life became a series of monotonous days for Angel. The lack of news from either Cutter or Stray left her with an empty coldness inside, as she grew heavy with child. She found a position with the Philadelphia Inquirer, as a freelance reporter, and went back to work under an assumed name. Toni helped her find a place to rent, also under an alias, and she began to settle into a new, if unsatisfactory, routine.

Although Ace contacted her every other day, Angel began to loose hope that Cutter would be found. Perhaps he didn't want to be found. The way he'd stalked away from her at the Florida campground, the anger he'd displayed in his posture, led Angel to believe that he could have disappeared on purpose. She found it hard to believe that his all-important mission could be so easily deserted; yet it was easier to think that he'd abandoned her, than to believe that the greys had caught up to him at last. The idea that he might be dead was far too horrible to bear. It was just so much easier to believe that he'd deserted her.

So she started a new life with a new name, the prospect of being a single parent uppermost in her mind, grateful for the sense of normalcy that came with no longer being on the run. The greys hadn't found her, couldn't find her, and she was almost able to believe that the running was over. If she wasn't six months pregnant with Cutter's baby, she might have thought she'd dreamed the whole damned thing.

Until her water broke.

* * *

Cutter came to in a state of confusion. His right shoulder was a blaze of intense pain, and he did his best to cut his mind off from the throbbing heat of infection, where he'd been run through with the pike. He lifted his head, tried to take stock of his situation. He was sitting, his wrists cuffed behind him to a chair. He was no longer blindfolded, but the darkness of the room prevented him from seeing anything of his surroundings. Where was he? More importantly, where were his captors?

Thought of Kowalski and the biomek suddenly brought his memories rushing back, and he almost groaned aloud. The two of them had taken turns interrogating him for what seemed to have been weeks, never letting him rest for more than an hour at a time, and after a while they'd become violent. They wanted Angel.

Cutter was proud that he hadn't told them anything. Not that he knew where she was, but he hadn't told them even that much. They'd kept him blindfolded, so that he couldn't influence Kowalski with his Will. The human had performed most of the violence, the biomek bringing Cutter around each time he'd passed out.

Eventually they seemed to have given up, and after days of torture, had finally allowed him to rest. He must have slept most of the night, and his eyes now detected the faintest lightening of a rectangle directly across from his position. A window?

In time the room itself began to brighten, and Cutter realized with a start that he was being held prisoner in Angel's mountain cabin! As the sun came up, and the room grew brighter, he saw that he was not alone. Ellem Ennopy stood in the doorway, studying him with cold eyes. When he realized that Cutter had regained consciousness, the biomek came into the room. He came over to stand above his captive, and said, "How do you feel?"

Cutter forced a grin. "How do you think I feel?"

"Do you require water?"

Cutter's grin vanished. What kind of game was this? He licked his lower lip and gulped in a dry throat, but said nothing.

Ennopy said, "Why don't you just tell us where the woman is?"

Cutter turned his face away, his jaw tight. It wasn't over, then. But the biomek had gotten rid of Kowalski. What did that signify? Was this finally the End? He found himself hoping it was. He couldn't live without Angel's love, didn't want to live without it.

All of a sudden, thoughts of Angel evoked a strange feeling within him. A dull ache, which threatened to become something more ominous. He gulped as realization set in, and a kind of panic overtook him. The Withering had come, as he'd known it would. He only hoped he'd have enough strength left to take it like a man.

"What's the matter?" asked the biomek, watching him closely.

"N-nothing." Lied Cutter, fighting a sudden and intense cramp somewhere inside. He knew that it would be worse in the beginning, but that the muscle spasms would ultimately lessen as his internal organs began to dry up and cease functioning, poisoning him in his own body. Another cramp doubled him over on the chair, intensifying the pain in his injured shoulder as his arm pulled against its restraints, and this time he inhaled sharply, his face twisted in agony. A word escaped him, despite his efforts to squelch it. *"Angel!"*

Ennopy simply watched, a slow grin spreading across his cyborg features. Very soon, Steele would reach out with his Will and seek his mate, and the greys would have her at last.

Chapter 13: Special Deliveries

The tinkling of breaking glass woke Cutter. He was still bound to the chair in Angel's kitchen, but found that he was alone in the semi-darkness. After another bout with Ennopy, he'd passed out again, and had been having deliriously mixed-up dreams of Angel. The sound brought him back to full consciousness, and he lifted his drooping head to look in the direction from which it had come.

He saw a hand poke through the broken pane of the front door, and reach around to unlock it. A moment later, Stray was standing over him, taking in his situation and condition.

"Cutter! Can you hear me?" He bent closer. Steele was in bad shape.

"Sssssss-- tray." He managed hoarsely. His head whirled, and the fever raging through his body made him sound dull and disoriented, even to himself.

"I'm going to get you out of here." Said Stray, already taking some tools from his jacket pocket. He began tinkering with the locks on the handcuffs which bound Cutter's wrists to the ladder-back chair.

Cutter felt dazed. Was this really happening? How had Stray found him? He'd left Stray with Angel and Ace in Florida, what had made him return to Angel's cabin in PA? Where was Ennopy? Any moment and the biomek could come in and discover this attempt at escape. He tried to speak again. "Th'-- biommmmmm..."

"He's gone. I watched him leave. I've been waiting for a chance to get in here and get you." Stray had the cuffs off, and Cutter fell forward into his arms, weak and nearly delirious. "Can you stand?"

Cutter shook his head to clear it, and tried to get his legs under himself, feeling like he was moving in slow motion. Stray put an arm around him for support, careful of the festering wound in Cutter's right shoulder. "Come on," he said, "I've got a car outside--."

Cutter took a tentative step, then doubled over as severe pain shot through his body.

Stray, realizing the cause of his discomfort, said,

"Look, you're only in the beginning stages. If I can get you back to Angel quickly enough, you'll be ok—"

"Angel—" whispered Cutter, trying to focus.

Together they moved across the room to the door, crunching through the glass on the floor, and out onto the log porch. The last rays of the setting sun slanted across the porch, lighting their way, and they struggled down to the gray Nissan parked at the foot of the steps.

Stray helped Cutter into the passenger seat, then closed the door and went around to the other side. Cutter curled against the seat, his face tight, as Stray got in behind the wheel.

He said, "Hurry . . . Stray . . ."

But the other man hesitated. He said, "Cutter, I lost contact with Angel when I came back for you. Where is she? Can you locate her with your Will?"

Cutter's blood ran cold. He squinted through the pain and fever-haze, at the man across the car. It was inconceivable that Stray would lose contact with Angel despite his orders and, even in his condition, Cutter's whirling mind jumped to a dreadful conclusion.

"No . . . " he whispered half to himself, then cleared his throat and spoke more firmly. "*No.*"

Realizing that the deception hadn't worked, Ellem Ennopy slammed his hand angrily onto the dashboard, and morphed back into his own guise, feeling the heat rise within his cybernetic body. Every time he changed shape, his body's micro-reactor burned hotter, using up valuable power. This mission was shortening his lifespan. He turned and reached across Cutter to open the passenger door, spilling the other out onto the dirt driveway with a soft grunt, then climbed out of the car and went around to the other side. He grasped the half-conscious Cutter roughly by the shirt and dragged him over the dirt, up the steps and across the porch, through the broken glass and back into Angel's cabin.

* * *

Toni Russo put out the light, and headed toward the stairs. She'd planned on going to bed for a quiet night of reading, and was startled when a frantic knocking sounded on her front door. She wasn't expecting anyone, and the hour was late, so she was reluctant to answer. She crossed the living room, not turning the light back on, went to the door, and called cautiously, "Who is it?"

From the other side came a woman's anxious voice. "Toni? It's me, Angel!"

"Angel?" Toni unchained the door and turned the bolt lock, then opened the door to find Angel French on her stoop looking frazzled. Her normally well-kept hair was in disarray, and she wore her coat over a long nightgown.

She said, "Toni, please! You've got to help me!" In the dim light from the street, snowflakes were drifting onto the girl's shoulders, and she looked frightened.

The older woman stood aside. "Come in! What's the matter?"

"I think my baby's coming!" she sounded as scared as she looked.

"Are you sure?"

"My—water broke," explained Angel shakily.

"Good God," said Toni. "I'll get my coat, and take you to the hospital—"

"—No, you don't understand," said Angel, near tears. "I'm only six months pregnant—"

"Six?" Toni swore beneath her breath. This could be really bad. "Hon, you've got to go to the hospital—"

"OH!" Angel doubled up with a contraction, gritting her teeth. After a long moment, she straightened. "I don't think there's time. My contractions're two minutes apart."

"Oh my God," whispered Toni. They'd have to deliver it here. She reached for her cordless, and dialed 911.

As luck would have it, all the lines were busy.

* * *

The wailing saxophone of Pink Floyd's "Money" emanated from the Suburban, as Ace's window slid down at the tollbooth. He tossed a token into the basket, and then pushed a button and his window hummed back into position, sealing out the cold, moist winter air. He proceeded over the Ben Franklin into Philly, his windshield wipers swishing away the swirl of falling snowflakes. He was only minutes from Toni Russo's. She'd called him at work, only an hour earlier, explaining

89

Angel's condition. He'd left the building at the same time the snow started, and had begun his journey through the mounting storm to Philadelphia, thinking about the other news he'd just gotten.

The sudden message from Stray had not been totally unexpected, but its timing was. Ace had just hung up his work phone, after talking to Toni, when it'd rung again.

"Hello?" He was in a hurry, and almost hadn't answered it. He was glad he had. It was Stray.

Stray had said, "Disc-man."

It was one of their codes, and Ace breathed easier. "Stray? Where've you been?" They hadn't seen or heard from him since he'd left Angel's SUV at the Georgia/Florida border.

"Everywhere." He said wearily. "I've got a prize for the dog catcher."

Ace caught his breath. He'd found Cutter? He said carefully, "Is the package wrapped?"

"No." there was silence and then he went on. "I've gotta do a pick up."

Ace collected his thoughts. Stray had found out where Cutter was being held, but hadn't been able to rescue him. "Will you need help?"

"I think I can handle it. I've got some domestic aid. How are things there?"

So. Stray had found some human assistance. Interesting. But there was important news on this front, as well, and Ace blurted, "I was just on my way out—I'm, er, going to a—'presentation'." He hoped Stray would get the message, and there was a long moment of silence before the other replied.

At last Stray said in a choked voice, "You're kidding. It's too soon." Was it really possible that Cutter's child was about to be born? After all of their people's plans and preparations, was their dream about to become a reality? It was too soon for a human pregnancy to be ending, but right on time for one of their own. He hoped everything was all right; this birth meant everything to their people. It would be their first success. He said, "Better get some 'watch dogs'." Angel and the baby would need bodyguards.

"I know. I will. And I'll pass along your information —"

"—No!" Stray's voice was urgent. He had no idea what had been happening to Cutter for the past month and a half, but the possibilities were grim, and he didn't want Ace to get Angel's hopes up, especially if she really was in labor. He said, "Wait until I have more to go on."

"Sure." Said Ace. "I'd better get going—" Toni had sounded desperate, and the weather was looking bad. He wanted to get over there as soon as possible.

"Yeah," agreed Stray. "I'll be in touch."

Ace had left work, and was just clearing the Ben Franklin's ramp; singing along with Pink Floyd, when Stray called again.

* * *

With one last, mighty push and a surge of fluids, Angel delivered Cutter's son into the world. An overwhelming feeling of triumphant joy washed over her, and the sounds of her son's bawling reassured her even further. Toni wrapped a terry towel around the crying infant and handed him to his mother.

"He's –so small," said Angel in an awed voice. Tiny but perfect. At only six months, he should have been in immediate danger but, except for his small size, he seemed as normal as a full-term baby.

Toni said, "I still can't get through to the paramedics—" They were in Toni's small, upstairs guest room, but she carried the cordless with her, and had tried repeatedly to reach 911. Outside, the weather had turned nasty, a late March snowstorm making the roads hazardous, and several accidents had been reported. Perhaps the emergency crews were all busy. Inside, the room was warm and dry; it's floral wallpaper and antiques a cheery backdrop for the drama that had just unfolded.

"It's ok," said Angel distractedly, staring into her baby's eyes. They were the almost-white paleness of Cutter's eyes, and amazingly focused. She found herself saying, "We won't need the paramedics after all. Toni, thank you. You're all we needed."

Toni shook her head. "Angel, you've still got to be

91

checked. The Baby has to be checked—"

She began cleaning up the soiled sheets and towels. She had known very little about delivering a baby, yet everything had gone as if they'd practiced. The infant was premature, yet perfectly formed. It was almost miraculous. She crossed herself, and began again. "Hon, you'll need a birth certificate and—"

But Angel didn't appear to be listening. She was staring down into her baby's face, and it seemed that the baby stared back. He was totally silent, now, watching his mother's face, regarding her in a way no infant should.

Angel said, "There'll be no certificate." She gave the other woman a look that said that this was her conscious decision, and Toni suddenly caught on. Angel couldn't register the baby because the greys would be looking for them. Ace hadn't explained these details when he'd brought Angel here, and Toni all at once understood their need for secrecy. Just then, there was a knock on Toni's front door, and she hurriedly left the bedroom to go downstairs and answer it.

Alone, Angel propped herself up on Toni's bed, then offered the baby her breast, and he began to nurse for the first time. The bond between them was immediate and almost telepathic. She'd sensed his hunger, as though he'd communicated it to her. Maybe he had. Those strange pale eyes were so like his father's...

"Yo!" said a voice from the doorway. Then, seeing that she was nursing, "Oh! Uh, Sorry, uh—"

"It's ok, Ace." Said Angel. "Come on in." she wasn't embarrassed by her activity, and didn't want him to be either. Nursing her child was only natural.

Ace entered the room, but kept his eyes carefully averted, his pudgy countenance a bit nervous. "How are you doing, kid?"

"Fine. We're both fine. Any news on Cutter?" Although she tried to keep the hope out of her voice, Angel didn't manage it. She gazed back at her baby, Cutter's baby, and thought her heart would break over his absence. He'd missed the birth of their son, so important to his mission, and even more so to himself.

Covington cleared his throat, hesitating. He didn't

want to lie, but didn't want to give her false hope, either. He said, "I heard from Stray--."

"Where is he?"

"Wouldn't say. But he had some information—"

"Tell me, Ace!" Why was he hesitating? Was the news that bad? "Is—is Cutter dead?"

"We don't know, yet. Word has it the biomek got him." He'd spoken again to Stray, on his way over here, and the news hadn't been optimistic.

Angel's face fell. The biomek. The biomek had killed both Fox and Boomer. She bit her lower lip, trying not to cry. She said, "Has Stray given up, then?"

Ace heaved a deep sigh, looking around the tiny room. He studied the flowered wallpaper, the antique dresser and ancient radiator. Finally he said, "One way or the other, Angel, Stray'll bring Cutter home."

* * *

The world around Cutter Steele exploded into brilliant light, and it occurred to him, somewhere in the midst of his delirium, that the biomek had finally decided to hand him over to the greys. He'd had enough of this world, and even though he looked forward to his coming death and dissection as a release from physical torment, every part of him rebelled at the idea of becoming an array of specimens in the grey's growing collection.

A loud rumbling shook Angel's cabin to its foundation, jarring Cutter into meager awareness. Noise and light and movement surrounded him. He could make no sense of any of it, captive of his own inner chaos. Events lost their natural order in time, and became a jumble of non-sequential incidents and anachronisms. His body shuddered spasmodically, in the midst of his hormonal withdraw, and the fever he suffered from his infected wound induced paranoid delusions that scurried around his brain like the drugged hallucinations of an addict.

Greys seemed to be everywhere. They swarmed around Angel's cabin in the brilliant glare, their nasty black eyes haunting his visions. His mind whirled, and he closed his eyes, shutting out the chaos surrounding him, but he could still feel the presence of the greys. Some of his own people were there; he could feel them too, as though he somehow had extra powers of perception. There was some kind of commotion or conflict, and he struggled against the wave of dementia that held him locked in confusion, blocking him from total awareness of what was taking place. He reopened his eyes. The biomek was hovering over him. It extended an arm that became a tentacle that attached itself to Cutter's forehead. He tried to push at it, felt himself restrained, and looked into the biomek's eyes. But suddenly they were the large black eyes of a grey. He tried to make sense of what was happening around him, but was no longer able to focus on anything beyond the light and noise and the pain of the muscle spasms that wracked him. His grip on reality was tenuous at best, and he felt himself sinking away from any connection with the real world, when Stray's face suddenly appeared within his field of vision. It was full of urgency and movement. Cutter shrank from the visage, muttering and moaning in his delirium, and finally fell back into the merciful numbness of total unconsciousness.

* * *

Angel paced back and forth across Toni's small living room, the baby asleep in her arms, waiting for any news of Cutter or Stray. It was days since Ace had announced that Cutter had been located. She'd slept at Toni's after the delivery of her baby and, after almost a week of resting and caring for the infant, she felt much stronger, but not at all relaxed. She wanted to be back in her own home, with Cutter and their child. Toni was a doll, helping her care for the baby, but it just wasn't the same, and Angel was aware of the differences. She wanted Cutter. She needed him. During their separation, her love for him had grown so strong, that she felt she could almost sense him. Somewhere in the cold March night he was on his way back to her, she could feel it. It was just a matter of time. But the endless waiting was beginning to wear on her nerves.

The baby stirred, as though sensing her inner anxiety. She patted him comfortingly, and he settled down. Thus far, she had refused to give Cutter's son a name. When pressured by others, she had stubbornly insisted on waiting until the child's father could help her choose.

The days following the baby's birth had turned bitterly cold, and the snow which had fallen still coated the streets, piled high where plows had come through, making the already narrow streets almost impassable. Angel stared out the front windows of Toni's home, the street lamps reflecting coolly off the mounded snow, and caught a movement. Across the street, a man walked the block, a dark shape against the white. Ace Covington had assigned several operatives to watch the house, insuring the safety of those inside. She sighed, wishing for a normal life again, but realizing that a life that included Cutter and their child would never be "normal". The best she could hope for was Cutter's safe return.

She never expected that Stray and his associates would carry him into Toni Russo's house later that night, unconscious and near death.

* * *

Cutter hobbled into the small conference room leaning heavily on a cane. His usually bronze face was haggard and pale, mottled with an assortment of cuts and bruises, his features tight. Behind him, Stray entered looking watchful. They were in an office building in downtown Philly, not far from the waterfront. The room was narrow and rectangular with a long table surrounded by comfortable chairs and matching vertical blinds. On the wall, a clock read just after 7pm. Beyond the windows, the city street was cold and deserted, the evening blackness relieved only by street lamps. It was after hours, and the group of men seated around the conference table were not executives, but a collection of operatives from around the East Coast who had been called to this spontaneous meeting only hours earlier. Cutter studied them as he entered, his almost white eyes still intense, missing nothing. He threw his Will at them, as was their custom, and felt their answering responses. Some of the men he recognized, others were strangers. All of them looked puzzled, and a hush had descended on them when he'd entered.

He took his place at the long wooden conference

95

table, Stray helping him to get seated, and then glancing around the faces of his associates, forced a wan grin. He cleared his throat, said, "Gentlemen."

Exclamations erupted, as though they'd all just found their voices.

He waited patiently until the noise died down, then addressed them. "First, I want to thank all of you for the effort and expense you put into my rescue. Stray and his men never could have made the attempt without your support." They'd supplied the money, weapons and equipment; Stray and his men had provided the information and the manpower. They'd searched for him from the time Stray had left Angel and Ace, and had located his whereabouts only a few hours before the biomek had contacted the greys and agreed to transfer Cutter to the their ship. Luckily Stray and his men had made their move before the transfer could take place, or Cutter wouldn't be sitting here now. If he'd been put aboard the impregnable ship, he never would have come out alive. He thought for a moment, about how close it had been. The greys had already invaded the cabin—

He shook his head to blot out the disturbing half-memories, and continued, "Second, I come to you tonight, with burdensome news. The—" He cut himself off sharply, shutting his pale eyes, as pain swept over him. The effects of his withdraw had been more intense a few days ago, but they were still powerful enough, and he rode the crest of agonizing sensation, struggling not to show it. On the way south to Philadelphia, Stray had insisted that Cutter join Angel first, before attempting this conference, but Cutter had been adamant; it was that important. He mustered his strength, said, "--The greys have called your effort to rescue me an attack against them. They condemn this attack as an act of war, and have 'officially' declared war on us." They'd forced the declaration into his brain, through a thought device, an invasive act he'd confused in his delirium with the biomek and its tentacle. Until now, the actual memory had been inaccurate and confused. He frowned at the way they'd used him, and then continued, "Gentlemen, they're going to throw everything they have at us."

For a long moment, no one said anything, as the full meaning of Cutter's words sank in. Then, for the second time, the room erupted into shouts and expletives. The greys were technologically far more advanced than anything they could muster and whatever their human allies could offer.

Stray sat at the long table, taking in the scene, and watching Cutter in particular. He saw his jaw tighten, his hands grip the edge of the table, white-knuckled, and knew what it was costing his friend just to be here. He let the shouting go on for a minute or two, then stood, and addressed the men.

"Cutter's right. From what we've learned recently, the greys have built themselves an army of their biomeks, and they're going to use them. Openly." He heaved a weary sigh, remembering the information Cutter had given him on the snowy ride south from Angel's cabin. There were more biomeks in existence than any of them had guessed, and the greys were no longer satisfied to use them only in private. He said, "It could escalate into public massacres, like the old mob wars we've learned about. The humans won't recognize it as anything more than that, but we're in danger of being slaughtered." He waited again, watching Cutter. He didn't want to take any more time than was necessary with this meeting; he wanted to get his friend back to Angel. He cut into the uproar and said, "We do, however, have some information which might be of some use. Cutter?" He sat back down, giving the floor to Steele.

Cutter forced himself up, leaning on his cane for support, and grinned his best arrogant grin. "The biomeks have a weakness." He told them quietly. In the sudden stillness of the room, the clock on the wall could be heard ticking. Now that he had their undivided attention, he went on. "When the biomeks morph, their body temperatures spike. We may be able to use this elevated temperature to track and target them. Ace is working on a possible method to utilize this information. It may even provide us with a way to——-" He cut himself off again, and everyone in the room waited patiently for him to continue. They knew what he was going through, and sympathized. Any one of them could face the same ailment, should their pair bond be broken.

He bowed his head to hide what he was feeling, gulped, and after a long moment, spoke. "I'm sorry. I--uh --Until now, we've been passively resisting the grey's attempts to wipe us out. But now, as I was saying, the-- um—the--." He suddenly found that he'd lost his train of thought, and his words faltered. His hands and knees had begun to shake, his mind whirled with fever, and he sat down abruptly. He glanced away from the table, dizzy and confused by his sudden lack of focus. He began again, "If we take the offensive with this new information--," he stopped, his hard features pale.

The man to his right, an operative whose name he didn't know, leaned closer. "Cutter, we need you. But not like this. Go home and be with your woman."

He nodded wearily, suddenly acknowledging how spent he was, how close to losing control of his own mind and body. He needed Angel--

Picking up the thread of conversation, Stray said to the men at the table, "We'll keep you all informed of our progress in finding a way to track and fight the biomeks. In the meantime, any help you can give Ace along those lines would be greatly appreciated. You know how to contact him." He concluded the meeting, leaving most of the men to discuss what had been said, then turned and helped Cutter to his feet.

Cutter gathered what strength he had left. He nodded briskly to those around the table, then turned and left the conference room, his cane supporting him. He made his way beside Stray and a few others, down the short corridor, and through the double doors.

He'd made it. His show of bravado would inspire the rest of the Resistance to fight harder. He'd risked everything to attend the conference, and had beaten the odds.

Outside in the icy parking lot, the air was brisk and cool, and Cutter breathed deeply. For a second he felt much better, just to be out of the stuffy building, but the moment the heavy doors swung shut behind him, his resolve wavered. Before he could reach Stray's Jaguar, he'd collapsed.

Toni Russo's row house wasn't far from the offices where the meeting of the resistance operatives had taken place. Moments after they'd gotten Cutter into Stray's car, they were pulling up outside of the block of brick homes. Lights emanated from several windows along the row, some of them the flickering glow of television sets, and a nearby street lamp made a patch of light that brightened the steps in front of Russo's home. The men Ace Covington had assigned to watch the house, greeted them, assisting Stray in getting Cutter out of the back seat, and carrying him between mounds of snow, to the top of Toni's stoop.

Angel herself answered their knock.

"Stray?" Her eyes widened in surprised shock, then glanced past him, to the two men who supported Cutter's unconscious body between them. *"CUTTER!"* She caught her breath, her gaze flying back to Stray, questioning.

Stray moved into the house, motioned the men to bring Cutter in. They put him on the couch in the small living room, as Stray was speaking to Angel.

"Where's Toni?" He surveyed the room, looking for the other woman, but didn't see her. It would be better if Angel were not alone with the news he had to give her.

Sensing what was coming, Angel said in a small voice, "Upstairs, with the baby—" she answered distractedly, going to Cutter's side. He was unconscious and badly bruised, his right shoulder bandaged under the coat he wore.

Stray took her arm gently, and turned her to face him. He said, "Angel, he's pretty bad off. The Withdraw has complicated matters, and we can't take him to a human doctor—," he let the words trail off, their meaning only hinted at.

Angel pulled away from him, and then bent over Cutter. Was Stray telling her that Cutter was dying? She ran a hand over his cheek, her fingers feeling the cuts and swellings, the heat of his fever. She cried, *"NO!"*

He couldn't die. She wouldn't let him. She loved him. Tears threatened to spill from her eyes, and she wiped them away, suddenly angry. All Cutter had wanted

99

was a family and a normal life here on this planet. What he'd gotten was a hounded existence and torture. And he didn't even know that he had a son. She straightened, turning back to Stray, her eyes blazing.

"He's going to make it, Stray; I'll take care of him. You take care of that damned biomek and the grey bastards who did this."

Chapter 14: Ties That Bind

April

Jeff Kowalski had returned to the boxing ring at the local Y. He found that it was the best way to take out his frustrations. He hadn't heard from Ellem Ennopy in several weeks, and the long wait was grating on his nerves. The blond, bearded foreigner had summoned him last month with a phone call.

"Kowalski? I have our 'friend'." There was gloating in his voice. "Would you like to exact a 'pound of flesh'?"

"Where are you?"

"The woman's cabin." Angel's place? Had Steele been stupid enough to go back there--?

"I'll be right there." He'd hung up, and gone directly to Angel's house, taking the interstate as he'd always done, when he'd been meeting her at the pizza shop. On the drive over, he wondered about Steele and Ennopy, and their strange connection. Supposedly, Steele had stolen the other man's wife and money, yet no wife had ever surfaced, no money had ever been recovered. If, by any chance, the woman was no longer alive, why hadn't Ennopy called the authorities? Had she even existed? Things just didn't seem to add up, and Kowalski had decided that perhaps it was better not to examine them too closely. After all, he and Ennopy pursued the same goal, and that was what mattered.

The familiar drive had also brought to Jeff's mind memories of the good times he and Angel had once shared, pastimes ground to such an unexpected halt by that damned stranger, Cutter Steele. All the possibilities for Jeff's own bright future had been ruined by some out of work gold-digger. He hated Steele for that. So, by the time he'd driven up the dirt driveway outside of her cabin, and parked next to Ennopy's gray Nissan, he'd been emotionally primed and ready for what he intended.

He'd arrived by four pm, the winter afternoon fading into dusk, and the setting sun had reflected off the recent snowfall, giving a certain warmth to the scene outside the log home. Inside, however, he'd found that the cabin was unheated and dim. Steele had sat slumped over on a kitchen chair, unconscious, his wrists cuffed behind him, new blood wetting the right side of his shirt. Ennopy had been standing at the front window, and turned as Jeff came in without knocking.

Skipping the preliminaries, Ennopy had said in a flat, dangerous voice, "I'll wake him. You can do whatever you like, just don't kill him."

Jeff grinned now, remembering his anticipation. He was going to beat Steele's head in, just like he'd envisioned. Ennopy had brought their prisoner around, while Kowalski removed his coat, preparing himself. His awareness of the low temperature in the cabin had soon faded, as he lost himself in his revenge, his own body warming with exertion. His blood lust had overwhelmed all his thought processes, as well as his sense of time. When Ennopy had finally hauled him back, away from Steele's inert and bloodied form, it had taken Jeff a few moments to collect himself, and remember where he was. He'd frowned, angry that Ennopy had stopped him.

But the taller man had spoken with a promise of future gratification. "Come back tomorrow."

He'd gone back almost every day for nearly two weeks. Some of the sessions had been short; others had lasted far into the night. Always, Ennopy had stopped Kowalski just short of doing any real, permanent damage. Jeff had wanted Steele dead, and resented the other man's restrictions. Steele might have recognized Kowalski's voice; it would be better to get rid of him. And besides, Ennopy had interrogated Steele between the beatings, but had never obtained the information he was seeking, so why prolong the inevitable?

In the end, Ennopy had sent Jeff home without allowing him to realize his deepest desire, to kill Cutter Steele. He'd promised to call him, when the time came to end the bastard's life, but so far the call hadn't come.

And so Jeff spent his spare time at the boxing ring, visualizing the end for Cutter Steele, and hoping he'd hear from Ellem Ennopy soon.

* * *

Cutter opened his eyes. He was lying on a bed in a small room with a high ceiling and tall, narrow windows. The walls were covered in floral patterned paper, and decorated with paintings of birds. The furniture was old, and the curtains made of lace, letting in the early morning sunshine.

Angel sat on a chair beside him, a shaft of sunlight tracing her features. Her face was toward him; her eyes had a far off look as she stared out the window behind him. Although she wore a slight frown, her dark features were beautiful nonetheless.

He spoke, his voice weak and groggy. "You really are . . . an angel . . ."

Her eyes immediately came back into focus, shooting toward him. "Cutter!" Her voice broke, and tears suddenly flowed down the curve of her cheeks. "I—thought —"

"Don't cry . . . Why are you crying?" The sight of her tears distressed him. He wanted to comfort her, but found that he didn't even have the energy to move.

"I was so worried! I thought—I thought you were-" she choked, putting her head down on his chest, wetting the blankets with her tears, and sobbing with relief.

"—dying?" He finished her sentence for her, and then forced a grin. "Huh! It'd take a lot more than one biomek . . . and a handful of greys . . . to take *me* out!"

His smile was cocky, the words self-assured, but she heard the effort in his voice. She sat up, giving him a closer inspection. Most of his cuts and bruises were healed, but many had scarred, becoming souvenirs of his torture. His face was thinner, making him appear a bit older, and there was a hardness to his eyes that hadn't been there before. His fever still raged, as his body continued to fight the infection brought on by his shoulder injury, and the terry washcloth she'd placed on his forehead had dried.

She took the rag from his head, rinsed it in a basin of cool water by the bed, and then replaced it, as she'd done for the past five days. The gentle touch of her fingers ignited an instinct within him that was so primal, so blindingly strong, that he was unable to stop it. His left

103

arm flew up, his hand catching her wrist in a fierce grip, his gaze locked on her face. Words tore from his throat in a deep, guttural growl, "I—need--you!"

Angel gasped. Stray had prepared her for this, warning her that, immediately upon awakening, Cutter would try to use his Will on her, his instinct for survival overwhelming all other protocols. He would have to renew their hormonal bond, in order to live. She had expected it, but not the violence it precipitated. He had her in a death grip, his gaze holding her hostage. She looked into his penetrating eyes, and it seemed that she looked into his very soul. She saw the war that was taking place within him, a battle between his heart and his will to live.

For a long moment, neither of them moved. Then, ever so slowly, Cutter released his grasp. He knew what Angel thought about his 'talent', knew that if he used it on her, even in this life-or-death instance, he could lose her. He relaxed his hand, and turned his face away from her, denying the powerful urge to use his Will.

"I shouldn't've done that." No sooner had the words passed his lips, than he was awash in a wave of painful withdrawal. He grunted, gritting his teeth. He said tightly, "If you—want out of this situation, here's your chance. Otherwise—"

She leaned closer, took his face in her hands, and turned it back toward her. "I understand," she said. "I love you." She kissed him, her soft, full lips pressing gently against his. As if by magic, the pain left him, flooded away by her warm nearness, and a ripple of pleasure surged through him.

It was too much to bear. He drew her down on top of him, clutching her tightly, returning her kiss with harsh desperation, until they were both breathless. He cried out, "Angel!"

First his Will, then his body; it was the only way to repair their Bond and save himself. He pushed her up a little, so that he could see her face. His eyes locked onto hers, thrusting his Will into her mind, despite a fear of what she might think of him later. "I'm sorry," he panted, " I can't help it! . . . I need you . . . I *have* to—"

"It's alright, Cutter, it's alright." She whispered,

feeling herself slide under his influence. Her breath became quick and warm against his neck. "It's alright…"

* * *

"The child is dead." Whispered the biomek into Cutter's ear. "The greys found your woman, and they took it from her. They killed it in their laboratories. We no longer need you, or your information. The child is dead."

Cutter woke with a start, his heart pounding heavily, his breath coming in ragged gasps. By the sunlight filtering into the room, he could tell it was late. Angel was gone, and he was left alone with the after-effects of the nightmare. Once the biomek had determined that physical torture wouldn't work on him, it had reverted to a more insidious form of persuasion: psychological games. After dismissing Kowalski, Ellem Ennopy had left Cutter alone for a day or two, and had then begun his new campaign. First, he'd disguised himself as Stray, and faked a rescue. When that hadn't worked either, he'd told Cutter that they'd found Angel, that they no longer needed him, and that he would soon be killed aboard the grey's ship. Shortly after that, the greys had once again appeared in Angel's cabin. Before he could be taken to their ship, however, the real Stray and his men had arrived. He couldn't remember much of the chaos that had followed, but the nightmare echoed reality. He lay bathed in sweat, in the small room, wondering where Angel had gone, and what had happened to their baby. Had the greys really killed his unborn child? It was obvious that his woman was no longer pregnant. He wasn't sure how long he'd been a prisoner in the cabin upstate, but he didn't think it had been long enough for Angel to have completed her pregnancy.

He stirred, realizing that it was the first time in weeks that he'd woken without being in the grip of tremendous pain, either from his hormonal withdrawl, or from the torture he'd endured. The aroma of cooking filtered into the small room, and his stomach rumbled. He couldn't remember the last time he'd eaten, either. He threw back the blankets, and sat up carefully, his injured shoulder still tender. There was a pair of men's sweatpants on the chair next to the bed. He pulled them

105

on, determined to find Angel, and left the room.

* * *

Angel had changed and fed the baby, then put him down for a nap in the portable crib in Toni's room. The older woman had taken care of the infant while Angel had been tending Cutter. When Toni had learned of Cutter's return to consciousness, she'd taken the opportunity to go on a weekend trip, leaving the family of three alone in her home, to bond.

Angel laughed silently at the expression, thinking of that morning. She and Cutter had renewed their hormonal bond at last, and now he slept, renewing his strength as well. He'd faded in and out of delirium for almost a week, and she'd feared that he would die, but his first lucid moments, his struggle to survive, had reassured her.

She puttered around the small kitchen, preparing dinner, and imagining what it would be like later, after she and Cutter and their child were together in their own home. Would they be free to live a normal life? Or would they be forever on the run from the greys? Would her son ever be truly safe?

A small movement caught her eye, and she looked up to find Cutter standing in the doorway, watching her. He was dressed in the new jogging pants she'd left out for him, his blond hair tousled, a badge of bandages marking the wound below his collarbone. His fever had broken and his bronze skin glistened with sweat. Despite his muscular frame, he was thin, and she was disturbed to see that he still needed to use a cane.

She said, "You're awake! What are you doing down here?"

"I missed you." He said simply, his voice low and meaningful, and his words caused the heat of arousal to rise within her. She put down the spoon she'd been using to stir some sauce, and went to him.

"How are you feeling?" she ran a hand over his naked, sweat-slippery chest. She touched the bandage. Concern edged her voice, despite her reawakened desire.

His expression hardened, and he said stiffly, "I'm fine." He attempted to stand straighter, to prove his words.

She glanced at the cane, said pointedly, "Are you?

Cutter, what did they do to—"

"I said, I'm fine!" he insisted harshly, not answering her question. He didn't want to think about what had happened up at the cabin. Would she really want to know the things her ex-boyfriend was capable of? He doubted it. Instead, he said gently, "Angel, we've more important things to discuss."

She felt a bit hurt, but dropped it. "Okaaay . . . For instance?"

He gestured around the kitchen. "Where are we?" He didn't recognize this place.

"Philadelphia. A safe house. It belongs to a friend of Ace, a very sweet woman named Toni Russo."

"Where is she?" As far as he could tell, they were alone in the row home.

"She's gone away for a few—"

"--Angel, you're no longer pregnant!" He blurted, interrupting. It was the most important thought on his mind, and he had to know: What had happened to their unborn child?

She grinned. "You just noticed?"

"I'm serious. Did--did the greys—"

"Oh, Cutter, no. No, of course not! —"

Right on cue, a cry sounded from upstairs.

"What's that?" he asked, taken totally by surprise.

Angel's grin widened. "That, Cutter Steele, is your son."

For a moment that seemed like eternity, Cutter just stood, paralyzed by her words. He opened his mouth to speak, but nothing came out. Finally he managed, "Wh-what did you say? My—son? You've given birth? I'm a father?"

Angel nodded wordlessly, still smiling. She took him by the hand, and led him through the kitchen and up the stairs, to see for himself.

* * *

The greys were not at all satisfied with the performance of their biomek, the one known on Earth as Ennopy. It had failed in its mission to locate and capture Angel French, and had allowed the escape of Cutter Steele as well.

107

Ennopy was well aware of their displeasure. As a reward for good service, the greys often replaced a biomek's micro-reactor, when its energy was near depletion. Ennopy's power was almost extinguished, and he knew he was in danger of termination. In his prior service to the greys, he'd been an excellent servant, and had survived the depletion of his energy twice when his masters had implanted new reactors. Things did not look good for a third renewal. If he couldn't deliver either French or Steele, or both, he was sure that he'd become just a pile of rotting bio-flesh.

After capturing Steele, Ennopy had copied the face of an operative he'd seen him with. During his attempt to fool Steele into believing he was being rescued, Ennopy had worn that face as a disguise, and Steele had put a name to the facade. He'd called Ennopy by the name "Stray". So. "Stray" was the name of one of the resistance operatives.

It was as good a place as any to start. Perhaps finding this Stray character would lead him to discover the new location of Steele and his family. He'd calculated the delivery date for Steele's offspring, and realized that the child must have been born already. The young of any species were especially vulnerable. A slow grin spread across his features.

Maybe taking the child, the carrier of Steele's and French's combined DNA, would redeem Ennopy in his creator's eyes. And, just possibly, it could earn him another energy renewal.

* * *

The church basement was large and well lit. As bingo players filed out after the night's games, a small knot of people hung back, gathering in the back corner, conversing in hushed voices.

News had recently broken, of a gangland style murder of several people in a restaurant in New Jersey. The papers were calling it the Palm Sunday Massacre, and attributing it to the Italian mafia. It was the third such killing in just under two weeks. True to Stray's prediction, the greys were openly using their biomeks to slaughter the resistance operatives and their allies.

Ace Covington joined the group of stragglers, throwing a light jacket over his shoulder. He said, "Hey, I'm not going to stick around. I've—uh—got somewhere to go."

"You're not hanging around to reap the glory of your success?" taunted Stray, studying the other's attire, and referring to the fact that Ace had come up with a way to track the biomeks. "You got a girl or something?"

"Well, uh, actually—" hedged Covington, rubbing a hand over his balding scalp.

"Anybody we know?" asked Toni Russo with a knowing smile.

"Uh, well," said Ace. "Yeah, you've met Nancy--"

"Ace!" Cutter grinned at his discomfiture. "You holding out on us? Have you bonded?"

"Not—not exactly," said the paunchy man defensively. "Maybe--maybe after tonight—I mean, on this world you're supposed to, you know, ask." He'd use his Will, of course, but only after he'd proposed to her. He'd been here long enough to know Earth customs.

"That's wonderful!" said Angel, giving him a quick hug. "I'm sure she'll say 'yes', and if she doesn't, she's a fool!" She'd met Nancy Carter a few weeks ago, a nice woman who wrote science fiction novels and stories for a major publisher.

Ace blushed. He said to Stray, "So, uh, you think you can sort of cover for me on this?" He was supposed to have presented his invention to the gathering of operatives tonight, and explain how they would use it to track their enemies.

Stray grinned. "Sure. I'll take the credit for you. Go have a good time."

Ace gave him a self-conscious grin, then moved off toward the exit and left.

At the same time, a middle-aged woman in a plain dress came into the basement from the steps leading up to the church, and addressed them all.

"Good evening, everybody. My name's Sister Mary Margaret. Father said we could use the basement after bingo, but we only have till eleven o'clock, so maybe we'd better get started?" Everyone took places at the tables,

109

and she scanned the small crowd, and then nodded to Stray.

Stray stood. "Thank you, Sister...I guess you've all heard about the hit in 'Jersey a few days ago." There were murmurs of assent, and he continued. "We lost four of our friends. Good friends." He bowed his head for a moment and then went on. "There were no shots fired, no weapons found. The FBI's investigating, of course, but we all know they won't find anything. My own human FBI partner believes that it was the work of the mafia. We know different. The greys have begun to step up their pogrom. They intend to wipe us out as quickly as they can using their biomeks. I called this meeting tonight to inform all of you of the progress in creating a tracking device. A device we will be able to use to locate the biomeks."

Angel tuned him out. She already knew about the device, from Ace himself. She glanced over at Cutter, sitting beside her, holding their baby. He still used his left arm most of the time, his right side not completely healed yet. He held the infant tenderly, his attention focused on his son's face. It'd been like that right from the beginning. He and their son had bonded instantly, and they were rarely separated from each other. Cutter cared for the baby all day, totally absorbed in fatherhood, while Angel worked.

She smiled to herself, remembering his shock when he'd learned of the baby's birth. When she'd taken him upstairs, to Toni's bedroom, to see his son for the first time. He'd stood in a kind of awed reverence, just staring at the baby, his pale eyes wide. Finally, he'd asked to hold him, and Angel had placed the baby in his father's arms.

"This is your daddy," she'd said to the infant, and when she'd passed him over, she was surprised to see tears on Cutter's cheeks.

Cutter had taken the baby, saying brokenly, "Angel —he's beautiful." The baby had coarse, curly blond hair, coffee-and-cream skin, and his father's almost-white eyes. Cutter had choked over a lump in his throat, his emotions almost overwhelming his ability to speak. He'd said, "This —I never dreamed—that this would finally happen. He's so beautiful..." He'd seemed too overcome to continue, but he did. "What've you named him?"

Angel had smiled. "I wanted to wait till we could decide together. Do you have anything in mind?"

"Matrix." He'd replied automatically, as though he'd given the matter much thought, and had decided long ago.

"Matrix?" Matrix Steele. It had a good sound.

Cutter had stared down at his son, much as he was doing now, and explained. "He's just the beginning, but he carries the seed, Angel, of a new species. He's the matrix, the mold, of a whole new race..."

When Angel came back to attention, Stray was just finishing his explanation of Ace's tracking device. "The problem is," he was saying, "that we won't be able to actually track biomeks until they morph. Which is usually when they're in attack mode." Grumbles broke out, and he said, "I know, I know. It's not good enough. But it's all we've got for now, folks, so I suggest we use it." He paused. "There's another matter I wanted to discuss tonight. Many of you have been suggesting that we vote-in an earth-side leader to our resistance efforts. The authorities on our home world have agreed. Only one name has been repeatedly mentioned for the position, both there and here: Cutter Steele. Cutter, will you respond?"

Still holding his son, Cutter glanced up sharply, caught off guard. Those around him urged him to reply. He handed the baby to Angel, and stood, still using a cane for support.

He thought for a long moment before speaking. He said, "As most of you know, I've just become a father." There were catcalls and whistles of support. "Across this world, the dreams of our people are finally being realized through our breeding mission." Applause interrupted him, and he waited for it to subside before continuing. "I love my family more than I can say. I don't want to endanger them or myself by being more active in the resistance." Again he hesitated, and the room fell silent, full of disappointment. "However, to keep my family safe, I'd do anything. I *will* do anything."

Angel sat, holding the baby and watching Cutter, her breath held. She didn't want to share more of her

111

family's time with the resistance, didn't want to lose Cutter to intrigue and plots. She wanted a normal life—

Cutter looked directly at her, at Matrix in her arms, then looked away, his jaw tight. He took a deep breath and said, "If tying myself to the leadership of this resistance furthers our cause, then so be it. I intend to fight for my child's right to grow up without being hunted and killed. I would give my life, so that my family—so that all of our families--will one day be safe and free."

Chapter 15: Fatal Distractions

Cutter tossed and turned, groaning in his sleep. His pale eyes shot open and he lurched to a sitting position, his heart hammering against his ribs, the breath catching in his throat. Sweat collected between his shoulder blades and beaded on his upper lip.

Angel, feeling the disturbance, woke and rolled over.

"Cutter? Are you alright?"

It was still dark in their bedroom, and she saw with blurry eyes that the clock's LED display read just after 4 am. What was he doing awake so early?

"Cutter?"

He took a deep breath and steadied himself, then said, "It was just a dream . . . go back to sleep."

His nightmares had become a regular occurrence that he adamantly refused to discuss. Angel rolled over, drifting back into slumber, secure in the knowledge that at least he was physically all right.

He sat there for a long moment, collecting his thoughts, and trying to calm his racing heart. The nightmare had been a particularly bad one, and he shook his head in the darkness, attempting to dispel its hold upon him.

He got out of bed, and limped into the bathroom, his bad leg stiff. He switched on the light and stared at his reflection in the medicine cabinet mirror, seeing the scars on his tanned face as if for the first time. The nastiest one curled around the outside of his right eye, and extended down along his cheekbone in an ugly, irregular white line. Below his collarbone, a mass of puckered white scar tissue signified the place where the biomek had run him through. He winced at the recollection, then turned on the faucet and splashed cool, foul-smelling Philadelphian water onto his face, in an effort to cleanse himself. To rid his memory of the torture he'd endured in Angel's cabin upstate, and the nightmares it had spawned. The greys' biomek and his cohort had been experts, careful not to kill him, but doing enough physical and mental damage, to leave him scarred in more ways than one. He sighed, knowing it was useless to try to erase the marks, but tired of waking in a cold sweat, and sick of being obsessed with looking at those damned scars. He turned off the tap and stared at himself again.

"You're better than this." He told his reflection firmly. "Tougher. Move past it." But, although his training had included ways to survive interrogation and torture, it hadn't dealt with how to handle the after-effects that now plagued him.

He pulled the shower curtain aside and turned on the water. As steam slowly filled the small room, he began to think a little more clearly. He forced his attention away from dwelling on the nightmare and its causes, and began to review his plans for the day. He had a meeting of operatives to attend, over on Delaware Avenue.

Ace had come up with a prototype-tracking device, but it hadn't been field-tested. They had to find some way of completely testing it, before they could manufacture and distribute more, and Cutter had come up with a plan. He climbed into the hot shower, considering the consequences should that plan fail. Worst-case scenario, someone would die. He felt a constriction in his chest at that thought. They couldn't afford to lose even one of their people, yet someone could die.

His jaw tightened in determination. There was no other way. He soaped a washcloth and scrubbed roughly at his skin, hating himself for what he must do today, but hating the greys even more.

* * *

"The device has to be tested. We can't usually measure the electrical trace of a biomek; it's too close to a normal human's. But, if the tracking device can pick up the energy signature of a morphing biomek, when it's temperature is elevated and the radiant energy is enhanced, it can record that signature, and then we'll be able to track them anytime, anywhere. The problem is, someone has to get close enough to a biomek while it's morphing. We need someone who knows both the device and the abilities of the biomeks." He gave Ace Covington a pointed look. "I'm not going to ask for volunteers. There's only one of us who's thoroughly qualified for this mission."

The old brick firehouse echoed with his words, underlining them, and Cutter winced inwardly. He didn't like sending anyone on such a dangerous mission, let alone a good friend.

Ace shrugged, trying to look indifferent. "Yeah, well, I'm the only one familiar with the new equipment. And I know where one of the meks has been hanging out. I'm pretty sure I can spot it, and get its trace signature."

Cutter nodded, glad Ace was accepting the assignment so readily. "You'll be our bait." And he took the paunchy man aside to fill him in on the details of his plan.

They had just finished speaking, as Stray came around the back of a ladder truck. Ace departed to prepare for his mission, and Cutter turned away, a tight look on his face. He started toward Stray, but another operative, a tall man in his mid twenties, interrupted him.

He approached Cutter, scowling, and said loudly, "You can't send Ace on this mission! He's just been pair-bonded!"

"Don't you think I know that?" said Cutter in a harsh, strained voice. He didn't need this kind of dissention right now.

"Don't you care? You've had time with your woman, Ace deserves the same."

"Do you doubt for one instant that I would go myself, if I –" Cutter stopped, swallowing hard. He'd almost said, *If I could.* He glanced down at the cane in his left hand, his pale eyes becoming slits of venomous hatred, and then he flung it angrily against the wall, the violent impact splintering it.

The young operative flinched and backed away from Cutter's rage.

Stray, who had witnessed the incident, came over and spoke calmly. "Cutter, we all know you'd go yourself, if you were able to. You crazy son-of-a-bitch, you'd probably even *enjoy* baiting the greys."

Cutter turned to his friend, and spoke angrily. "I'm sick of letting you and the others do all the dirty work, take all the risks to defend our families, while all I do is—"

115

"—is make all the hard decisions," cut in Stray, "and live with the consequences. You fight the greys in your own way, Cutter, and no one thinks any less of you for it. That guy's just a kid who's feeling idealistic and passionate. You've already paid the price once. We know that."

Steele heaved a weary sigh. He said, "But the price I paid wasn't high enough, was it?"

For answer, Stray patted him on the shoulder and walked away.

* * *

Angel threw things into her overnight bag as quickly as she could, now and then glancing out the second story window, watching for Cutter. She'd given him a lift downtown, on her way into work this morning, and had expected to find him already here when she'd arrived. Instead, she'd found Toni Russo still watching Matrix. Toni was downstairs now, playing with the baby as Angel packed. She'd received an email on her computer at the newspaper, from the woman she used to work for. The state police had been looking for Angel, to let her know that her cabin had burned down. The insurance company hadn't been able to reach her, either, and had sent investigators to find out what had happened to her following the Meteor shower. Her former boss had said that Angel had been reported missing and presumed dead in the disaster, until she'd recently contacted her by email.

As she tossed some makeup into a second bag, Angel saw a dark blue Saturn pull up in the alley behind their garage. Cutter got out, and made his way into the garage, as the car pulled away. "I really ought to teach him to drive," she said to herself. Although Cutter had a fake driver's license provided by one of the operatives in the bureau, he still hadn't gotten around to learning how to operate a car. Angel finished what she was doing, grabbed up her bags, and headed down the stairs to meet him.

Cutter stomped haltingly up the steps from their basement garage, knowing he was late, and wondering if Angel was home yet. Her Cherokee wasn't in the garage, but sometimes she parked on the road in front of the row home they were renting.

He was surprised to find Toni Russo still caring for Matrix, and Angel coming down from their bedroom, two overnight bags in her hands.

"What's up?" he asked, his eyebrows raised in question.

Angel gave him a quick kiss. "I have to go home."

Cutter froze. "Wh-what? Angel, you are home. Your home is here, with Matrix and me." Was she--leaving him? Why?

"That's not what I mean." Sometimes he could be so innocent, she thought. And she explained to him about the email she'd received.

Although relieved that she wasn't leaving him, Cutter immediately frowned. Angel had no idea what had actually happened to her cabin upstate. She had been told that it'd burned down, but the facts of the matter were far more complicated. Her cabin had been destroyed in the attempt to rescue him from the greys, and no one, not even the state police, knew the real details concerning the destruction of her home. They thought it was just meteor damage. He had to stop her from going up there, and finding out what had really taken place.

"If it's been destroyed, why bother? We have a life here, now."

"Cutter, that was my parents' home. It's where I grew up. I have to go—" She could see he didn't understand. He'd never had a real home, or a family. He'd been alone and on the run his entire life, and those things just weren't as important to him as they were to her. "I'm only going for the weekend—"

Toni said, "I can stay with Matrix, if you want to go with her, Cutter."

He'd almost forgotten that Toni was there. He considered the woman's offer. He couldn't let Angel go upstate alone. He said, "Thanks, Toni." To Angel, he said, "Can you at least wait for me to get a change of clothes?"

Angel grinned. They hadn't been alone together since Matrix was born. It would be like a mini-honeymoon. "Sure," she said, "But hurry. I want to get up there before

117

dark."

* * *

As Angel drove, the silence between them stretched. Cutter was unusually quiet, staring out the window of the SUV, his pale eyes looking far away. He hadn't been sleeping very well lately, and had been distracted and distant as well. That something was bothering him was obvious. As she pulled onto the interstate, Angel wondered what it was, and if she was going to be able to get him to talk about it on the two-and-a-half-hour drive.

She said, "Feels funny to be out together without Matrix, doesn't it?" The empty car seat in the back was a forlorn reminder that somebody important was missing.

"Hmmm?"

Angel's gaze shifted from the road, to Cutter, and back again. His pale eyes were glazed, his face drawn and a bit haggard. She said, "What's the matter? You seem worried. Toni will take good care of him."

Cutter rubbed his forehead, where a headache was threatening. How could he tell her that he'd just sent one of his best friends on what might turn out to be a suicide mission? He'd been making decisions like this all his life, and it'd never bothered him, until now. Why the sudden attack of conscience? Had becoming a family man made him more empathetic? Was it because he knew that Ace and his woman had just bonded? Was he feeling guilty to be going off for a weekend alone with his own woman? A sense of doom washed over him, and he choked it down before answering.

"I'm sure Toni will do just fine. She's a kind woman, and a good friend."

"What is it, then?"

Indeed, what was it? Why was he finding it so difficult to perform the duties he'd taken on, when he'd accepted leadership of the earth-side operatives? Why did things suddenly seem so complex and hard to deal with? He hadn't had a good night's sleep in weeks. Perhaps that's all it was. "Maybe I'm just tired..."

"Well, go ahead and rest. I'll wake you when we get upstate."

Cutter sighed, and put his head against the

window, closing his eyes. He didn't want to sleep. Didn't want to dream. But the confusion in his brain made it difficult to figure out what was bothering him, or to talk about it either, so he was relieved to escape Angel's questions by feigning sleep. If he could just sort it all out...

* * *

Cutter jumped awake with a startled yell, almost making Angel swerve off the road. She got the SUV under control, and turned to him, alarmed.

"Whoa! You ok?" She gave her attention back to the road, waiting for his reply, and comparing this scene to the night they'd first met, when he'd come to in her car.

He didn't answer for a long moment, his breath coming in quick gasps, his heart pounding. Finally he managed, "Yeah--yes. . . It was just a bad dream . . . I'm . . . fine."

"You've been having an awful lot of those lately." She commented.

Cutter said nothing, still trying to recover from the dream's affects.

"What're they about?" she asked timidly, concerned.

Should he tell her? Should he let her in on his private agony--the memories of what had happened up at the cabin? Would it reduce him in her eyes, if she knew he couldn't handle what had been done to him? If she knew it kept him awake, and haunted him whenever he did sleep? Should he tell her what plans the greys had had for him, if he'd actually been transferred to their ship? It would have made what Ennopy and Kowalski did to him look pleasant.

He said carefully, "They're just dreams. They don't mean anything."

"Yes, they do." She countered. "They're destroying you, Cutter. Don't you see that?"

Again he didn't answer, and she drove in silence for a while, before trying another tactic.

"What happened at the meeting this morning?"

All of a sudden, he was angry. "I sent Ace on a possible suicide mission."

119

The deadly ferocity in his voice sent a chill down Angel's spine. She slowed for a tollbooth, and glanced his way.

"Why? Why Ace?"

"Because he was the best man for the job." He told her flatly. He didn't tell her that he would've gone himself, if his bad leg wouldn't have slowed him down. Didn't mention the humiliation he felt at having to send someone else to do his job for him. A *friend*, yet.

But Angel was figuring things out for herself. She said, "Do you really think it's that dangerous?"

Was there a chance that Ace would survive a biomek's attack? Cutter stared out the window, the sense of doom washing over him once again. Before he'd met Angel, he could have answered that question easily, objectively and without guilt, knowing that their mission took precedence over everything. Now, he could only fight off an overwhelming pessimism and hope that Ace would make it.

* * *

Ellem Ennopy turned his gray Nissan onto the highway, and glanced at the map in his brain with his inner eye. After weeks of searching, he'd finally come across a reference to the operative named "Stray". The man was, astoundingly, an FBI agent based in New York. If he could talk to the man, convince him that he was a friend of the resistance; perhaps he'd learn the location of Steele and his family.

In the back of the gray Nissan, was an empty infant's car seat.

* * *

The Wrangler bucked as Jeff Kowalski banged gears leaving the parking lot of the local Y. He was in a foul mood, and had been in one all week. Ellem Ennopy had never contacted him, and despite several calls each day, he hadn't been able to get in touch with the foreigner. That morning, his call to the motel had been re-routed to the front desk, and he'd been informed that Ennopy had checked out.

He slammed his fist onto the dashboard, angry. The foreign bastard had used him to do his dirty work, and had then abandoned him without explanation. He scowled, changing gears as he entered the interstate, and thinking. Where would Ennopy go? Back to Angel's cabin?

He seriously doubted it. Ennopy, if that was even the man's real name, was probably already out of the country. What of Steele? Had the big man killed Cutter himself? That thought angered Kowalski the most. What if Ennopy had murdered Steele, depriving Jeff of that pleasure?

There was only one way to find out. He'd have to check the cabin. He took the exit onto I84, and headed toward Angel's place, not even seeing the familiar gray Nissan that passed him in the opposite direction.

* * *

The paunchy, balding man took his wallet out of his back pocket, and thumbed out some bills to the man in the admissions booth. Beyond the chain-link fence, go-karts sped around the oval track, stirring up clouds of dust and breaking the morning quiet with their whining roar.

He thrust his Will at the other, but got no response. It was like talking to a wall, and so he was sure he had the right person. He said, "How 'bout clearing the track and letting me do a solo run?" He knew it was against the track rules, but he was supposed to start an argument. Later, the money-taker should follow him, intent on a fight. A fight that would lead to a violent attack, requiring the biomek to morph. Only then would Covington be able to procure the important information he sought.

The man in the booth grinned, one of his front teeth missing. A nice touch, that missing tooth, it made him look more human. He nodded toward the sign. It showed a large pig, with the lettering, No Hogging the Track. He said, "You want to ride, you gotta join the others."

The balding man squinted into the morning sunlight, pretending to consider. He was going to start the argument by insisting, as Cutter had originally planned, but then thought of a better idea, a less dangerous way to get the mek to slip into morph mode. He said, "You race?"

The bigger man's grin widened. "Yeah, do you bet?"

Ace thumbed out more cash, making sure the other

121

saw the wad in his wallet. "Yeah, I can put up some stakes. When?"

"After closing."

Ace nodded, then walked away, knowing that the biomek must have made him as an operative. So. They both knew the real stakes.

* * *

By early the next afternoon, all of the insurance papers had been dealt with, Angel's old bank account had been closed, and Angel and Cutter found themselves free for the rest of the day. They stopped at a local restaurant for some lunch, and sat in a booth waiting to be served.

Angel said, "When we're through here, I want to stop by the cabin and see how badly it was damaged."

Cutter's face drained at the idea. He didn't want to go back to that place. He'd do almost anything to get out of it. Except tell Angel.

He said, "Do we really have time? I thought you wanted to get back on the road." He forced a grin. "You know, get back home to Matrix."

Angel reached across the table, and took his hands in hers. "The state police think my cabin was destroyed in the Meteor shower; you and I know better. I want to know what happened after we ran away that night. This is . . . something I just have to do."

Cutter pulled back, folding his arms across his chest, steeling himself to do as she wished. "Yeah, ok." He understood her curiosity, but couldn't explain his reluctance to her, so he figured it would be best to just go along. Even if it meant going back there.

Their lunch came, and they ate in silence. Angel watched Cutter push his food around on the plate, disinterested. Usually he was enthusiastic about trying new Earth foods, but today he seemed apathetic and somehow nervous. Again she got the impression that something was bothering him. Could it be the mission that he'd assigned to Ace? Was he really that certain that his friend wouldn't come back alive?

She said, "Ace is one brilliant man. He can think himself out of almost any situation. I'm sure he'll be alright."

Cutter forced another smile, trying not to think about either Ace, or what they might find at Angel's cabin. What was the matter with him? His mind was overwhelmed with feelings of dread and doom. Emotions he'd never experienced before, and which he couldn't seem to control now. "Sure. Look, you ready?" He stood, picking up the check, in a hurry to move. Might as well get this done and over with.

Angel wiped her mouth with her napkin, grabbed her purse, and joined him at the register. They paid for the meal and left the restaurant.

* * *

Jeff hit his turn signal and turned off the ramp onto route 402. He made another quick turn, and then traveled the back road for some distance, preparing to make a right onto a dirt road. Up ahead, at the place where he was planning to turn, a white Cherokee was just entering the neighborhood, and sight of it caused the breath to catch in his throat.

Angel's SUV? Couldn't be. Yet, he found himself hoping.

By the time he approached the turn off, and had made his right, the Cherokee was already out of sight. He slowed his Wrangler, and proceeded along the dirt road, his heart skipping with nervous excitement. Halfway down the road, he pulled over and parked. If it really was Angel, he wanted to surprise her. He got out of the Wrangler, locked the door, and began to walk.

* * *

Sight of her destroyed home shocked Angel speechless. She circled the cabin, taking in the total destruction, wordlessly searching for an explanation. Cutter stood by the Cherokee, not invading her privacy as she explored the outside of her home. He felt rooted to the ground, unable to approach the cabin, inundated by memories he didn't want to recall. When she'd circumnavigated the place, and came back to his side, Angel was pale, and tears streamed down her cheeks.

"It's—gone! Everything—everything's gone..." her voice trailed off, sounding lost and bewildered. There wasn't much left at all, just the charred fireplace and its

123

chimney, and one corner of the front of the house. Remnants of some of the larger pieces of furniture stood, blackened, in the center of where the rooms used to be, like burnt sentinels, and were black with soot. The entire area still smelled of acrid smoke, even after all this time.

Her turmoil brought Cutter out of his daze. He shook off his own feelings of dread, and put an arm around her shoulders, drawing her close. "Come on," he whispered. "Let's take a walk." He grabbed up a sturdy tree branch to use as a walking stick, and they headed toward the tree line.

They moved into the woods, down the trail to the creek, scuffing at the dead leaves and weed choked path, Cutter hobbling along beside her as she attempted to deal with her loss.

Down at the creek, Angel let loose, and cried bitterly. Everything she'd had, every memento of her parents and her childhood, was gone. Cutter held her tenderly, loving her, wanting to comfort her, but not knowing how. After awhile, she sniffed, looking up at him, and tried to smile. "It doesn't really matter, does it? You and Matrix are all I need, now."

Cutter thought his heart would explode with joy at her words. He kissed her tenderly, a long, slow kiss that threatened to become more passionate. Angel returned his kiss, running her hands through the back of his hair, becoming aroused. Suddenly, Cutter stiffened, his pale eyes staring at something beyond Angel's shoulder. She turned questioningly, to see what he was looking at. There was something at the edge of the creek bank, lying half in the water. She dropped her arms from about his neck, and they both moved closer, puzzled.

Angel's mouth fell open, as she recognized the decomposed shape of a dog's body, the bones protruding through the dusty yellow fur. "A-Asti?"

Cutter pulled her away, the feelings of dread again washing over him in strong waves. "Let's get out of here." They made their way back to the cabin, Cutter's thoughts racing. So, the biomek had killed the dog here, before they'd ever even left for the shack in the Jersey pinelands. No wonder they'd been tracked so easily.

The sun was starting to get low as they came out of the woods. Angel cast one last glance back at the place where her cabin had once stood, and she caught her breath in a gasp. There, in the center of the blackened ruin, stood the lone figure of a man.

* * *

Ace pulled the steering wheel of the go-kart violently to the left, deliberately smacking into the other kart, trying to force it off the track and into a rollover. If he could injure the biomek, it would have to morph away the wounds, and he'd get the electrical signature he needed. The man behind the wheel, gave him a surprised look, then grinned and pushed his vehicle to the right, into Ace's. Ace let out a yell, and struggled to keep his kart upright. The battle had begun.

* * *

"Jeff?" Angel's voice was soft and puzzled. She hadn't seen Jeff Kowalski in so long that she almost hadn't recognized his shadowed, well-muscled shape. What was he doing here?

He came toward them, his gait graceful and confident, something dangling from his hands.

Cutter froze, his gaze locked on the thing in Kowalski's grip.

Kowalski glanced at Angel, and said softly, "Angel. Still so beautiful." Then, more loudly, "What're you doing with this piece of trash?" He grinned at Cutter. He held up a pair of sooty handcuffs, said, "Lose something?"

Cutter kept his eyes on Jeff, but spoke to Angel, "Get in the car." All at once, the sense of dread he'd been feeling had escalated. Things were about to get ugly, and he needed her safely out of the way.

Angel just stared at him. His breath was slow and deep, his features calm, but his eyes frightened her. Something was going on here that she couldn't quite grasp. There was a tension between the men that shouldn't be there, something more than just jealousy.

"Why?"

"Just get in the car!" he ordered, still keeping his attention on Kowalski.

Jeff's grin widened, and he shook the cuffs, making

125

them jangle, grating on Cutter's nerves. Spying something in the rubble, he tossed the handcuffs to the ground, and picked it up. From the litter of kitchen debris, he drew it, a dirty carving knife

Cutter eyed the weapon in disbelief. Did Kowalski think that would stop him? He locked his gaze on Kowalski's face and said, "Put that down."

Jeff paused, fighting a tremendous urge to drop the knife. He shook his head, clearing it, and reasserted himself.

"Don't be stupid, Steele, you know what I'm going to do with this. What I would've done before, if Ennopy hadn't stopped me."

Cutter was surprised by the human's strength of will, but pushed his own Will forward again. "I don't think so."

"What do you mean, you don't think so?" sneered Kowalski, his gaze meeting Cutter's.

"I think you're going to do yourself." He replied in a quiet, suggestive voice, his desire for revenge finally getting the best of him, washing over him in a powerful wave that flooded away even the feelings of doom.

Against his will, Jeff found himself putting the knife to his own throat, suddenly realizing that Cutter was somehow forcing him to do so.

His eyes went wide in panic. He gasped, and said in a choked voice, "What are you doing to me?"

"What are you doing to yourself? All's fair in Love and War, and this happens to be both." Cutter spoke evenly, feeling the power of his Will surging through him and being pushed into Jeff's mind. It was so easy.

"A little harder." He told the other cruelly, and the knife at Jeff's neck pressed more firmly into his throat, threatening to slit it.

All at once, Cutter felt Angel's hands on his arm, tugging at him for attention. She knew what he was doing, and couldn't let him continue. "Cutter! Cutter, *no!*"

He turned, hearing her at last. Her desperate words finally broke into his mind, which was dazed with emotions so strong he could barely control them. He wanted to give in to those feelings, to release the rage that he'd been holding back. He wanted revenge, and Angel was a distraction he couldn't afford.

"Please," he said, "For my sake, get back into the car!" He wanted to finish this here and now, but not with Angel looking on.

"Think about what you're doing, Cutter! Stop it, please! --Or were the greys right about your people after all?"

He looked from her to Jeff, all at once hesitant. His desire for revenge was so strong he felt nearly lost in its power. Yet, if he forced Jeff's hand, forced the man to kill himself, he'd be abusing his talent, and he'd lose Angel's love forever. He stood, his body tense, his eyes a smoldering blue fire, his breathing hard.

After a long moment, he backed off a step, his eyes still locked on Jeff's face. He took a deep breath, then blew it out, and spoke to Angel. "Alright, you've stopped me. I just hope you don't regret it later."

His attention wavered for an instant, and suddenly Kowalski was upon him, the knife still in his hand. They grappled, each man trained to fight, each one of them strong. But Kowalski knew the other's weaknesses. He kicked Cutter's bad leg out from under him, and then they were both falling—

Chapter 16: Life and Death

The go-karts sped around the dirt track, sending clouds of dust into the air and obscuring the racers' vision, their motors whining in protest.

Ace waited for the other driver to make his move. When he judged that the mek was just about to attempt another ram, he hit the breaks on his own vehicle. The opposing go-kart zoomed past, cutting in front of Ace at a dangerous angle. It hopped the tires lining the track, flew into the air, and then cart-wheeled across the track into the infield.

Ace applied his brakes harder, stopping his kart. He unfastened his harness, and leaped out of the car, then sprinted for the wreck. He knew that if the biomek had been injured, it would be morphing the injuries away, and that time was of the essence. On a cord around Ace's neck hung a small, tubular metal object. He fingered the object as he approached the damaged go-kart, his heart pounding.

Sure enough, the biomek's body was missing one of its limbs, and the head section had been bashed-in by the bending of the roll bar. It flailed its remaining arm, as it tried to morph, its actions impeded by the mutilated control center, which had been located in the biomek's brainpan. Ace pushed a button on the device at his neck, quickly recording the electrical output of the creature.

Satisfied that he'd gotten the necessary information, he sent the information over the internet, then turned to leave. And came face-to-face with the missing limb. It had taken the form of a large cat, and it leaped toward him, its metallic, razor-sharp claws and fangs exposed. It landed just below his shoulder, bowling him over and digging into his flesh, and as he screamed and struggled to dislodge it, the simulacrum began to tear at his throat.

* * *

Kowalski recovered from the fall first, the knife still in his hand.

As blinding pain shot through his bad leg, Cutter

labored to concentrate on the fight, and to keep the charred blade from slashing him. He had landed on the ground beneath Kowalski, and he fought the other man, trying at the same time to make eye contact with him, intending to use his Will if necessary, to win.

Jeff gulped in a dry throat, realizing too late that Steele was a much stronger adversary than he'd anticipated, and that defeating him would not be as easy as he'd expected. The kick he'd landed on Steele's bad leg didn't seem to have done as much damage as he'd hoped. He was tempted to check the other's features for some sign of the pain he should be experiencing, but he knew better than to look Cutter in the face again. He'd have to try something else.

He switched the knife to his other hand, a trick that he'd used with some success before. He'd trained himself to use either hand when fighting with a weapon, and hoped that the change would throw Steele off.

Although unprepared for the switch, Cutter nevertheless used it to his advantage. He twisted away from the weapon and sprang awkwardly to his feet, taking Jeff with him, and both men circled. The dry soot and ash covering the ground rose in a cloud of black powder around their feet.

Angel just stood watching them helplessly, unable to move. She didn't have to be told that this was a fight to the death, and tears of fear cascaded down her cheeks. She didn't want to witness any of this battle, but couldn't look away, afraid for both her ex-friend and for her lover.

Jeff lashed out with the knife. He missed, but was rewarded with the drag of resistance caused by Cutter's clothes. Spurred on by the possibility of triumph, he slashed again.

Cutter felt the nick of the blade, but ignored it, focused only on the pulse throbbing at the side of Kowalski's neck. Even as Steele evaded his opponent's jabs, he watched that vein, getting into its rhythm. When the man suddenly lunged at him, Cutter thrust his arm out straight, his knuckles in line with his wrist so that his entire arm would become a lethal weapon, aimed at Kowalski's chest. The timing was precise, the aim accurate. Jeff crumpled and dropped to the ground. The blow had caught him between heartbeats, as Cutter had intended, and the force of the impact had killed him instantly.

Cutter, still breathing hard from exertion, turned to Angel. "Go up the road . . . and use your cell phone . . . Call an ambulance, and then try to reach Stray . . . Tell him what's happened."

* * *

It was just getting dark as Angel pulled her Cherokee back into the drive at her burned out cabin, Stray's headlights behind her. They'd gotten to the scene ahead of the state police. Angel knew the way back into the woods around her home, but the troopers, relying on directions, had missed a turn and had had to back track. Stray parked his silver Jaguar behind her car, got out, and hurried to over-take Angel, a cell phone pressed to his ear.

She walked toward Cutter who sat on a tree stump, staring vacantly at nothing, Jeff's dead body sprawled on the ground before him. He hadn't touched anything, and the scene was the same as it had been when Angel left, except for the darkening sky and the jag's headlights. Stray caught up to her, putting his phone away and, taking her elbow in his hand, they approached Cutter together.

When they were within a few feet of him, Cutter looked up. His hair was tousled, his clothing dirty and torn from the fight. For a moment Stray thought Cutter's pale eyes held the look of a hunted animal. Then recognition transformed his features. He stood, and said to Stray, "Thanks for coming..."

Just then, the state police arrived, the lights on their car flashing. The troopers got out of the vehicle, and Angel and Stray left Cutter to go and greet them.

There were two staties, and the first one touched the brim of his hat as he addressed Angel. "Ma'am. I'm officer Seabrook; this is officer Demarco. We're responding to a call about an assault. I assume you placed the call?"

Angel nodded wordlessly, her dark eyes large, and tried to avoid looking at Jeff's body. "Th—that man attacked Cutter with a knife—"

"Excuse me, Officer." Stray took out his identification, and handed it to Seabrook.

"FBI?" said the trooper. "What do the Feds have to do with this?"

Stray nodded to the corpse on the ground. "This man was wanted in connection with an interstate abduction and assault."

"Abduction? Whose?" asked Demarco, speaking for the first time.

Stray indicated Cutter, standing over the body, his face pale but expressionless.

Officer Seabrook said, "Alright, we'll want to get statements from all of you. The ambulance should be here shortly." He addressed Stray. "Meanwhile, could you fill me in on the deceased?"

Stray said, "Him? Name's Jeff Kowalski. He's been working with a group who had abducted Mr. Steele. We saw him coming and going from the cabin when we had it staked out, and Cutter later identified him as the one who tortured him."

"Jeff?" Angel was aghast.

"Do you know him?" Asked Officer Seabrook, shifting his attention to her.

"Yes—he was an ex-boyfriend." She answered vaguely, feeling feint. Jeff had been involved all along? Why hadn't Cutter told her himself? "I thought I knew him."

"Then, I'm sorry for your loss." Said Seabrook tactfully.

Stray said, "I wasn't aware of your former relationship. I'm sorry."

But she could tell that Stray was glad to see Jeff dead. There was coldness to his demeanor that he usually reserved only for the greys.

The ambulance arrived, pulling around the police vehicle and other cars, and parked on the grass. EMTs jumped out, and immediately began to perform their duties. Darkness had fallen, and Stray watched them as they finally wrapped the body of Jeff Kowalski in a black plastic body bag. He'd told Angel about Jeff's part in the drama, unaware that she'd had feelings for the man, and now he had to tell Cutter about Ace.

He looked across the driveway, to where Cutter was standing alone in the flashing lights of the police cruiser, watching Kowalski's body being lifted into the ambulance. His face was set, unemotional, but there was a repetition in the clenching and unclenching of his jaw that alerted Stray. He excused himself from Angel and the trooper, and went over to his friend.

"Cutter? You alright?"

Steele's gaze shifted quickly to Stray, then darted away. "Of course."

"You'll be questioned by the authorities on our Home world about this."

"Of course." he repeated as flatly as before. Taking the life of humans was considered as heinous a crime as the murder of one of their own.

"I wouldn't worry about it. It was self defense."

"Was it?"

"Wasn't it?"

Cutter swallowed. "I don't know." His gaze finally met the other man's.

He said, "I--wanted revenge, Stray. Would've used my Will to get it."

"I know. But you didn't--"

"--Only because Angel stopped me. I wanted to kill him."

"You had no choice. He would have killed you just as quickly."

Steele looked away again, forcing himself to sound apathetic.

"Yeah. Ok. What else have you got?" He knew Stray had something more to say.

Stray hesitated. "Ace's mission was a success. He got us the energy signature we needed." He'd gotten a phone call regarding Ace's email, just as he'd arrived at the cabin. The caller had informed him of Ace's information about the biomek's energy signature.

Cutter's mouth pulled up at one corner. "Good. But--?" There was something the other man wasn't saying. When Stay didn't answer immediately, Cutter's jaw tightened again.

"Ace didn't make it, did he?"

Stray cleared his throat. "No."

Steele just nodded and turned away as flashing red and white lights announced the departure of the ambulance.

* * *

As Ennopy headed east into New York City, the sun sank below the western horizon, and the tinted membrane that had been protecting his eyes from the late afternoon glare off the skyscrapers, dropped back down. The traffic was slow and heavy, and the automobile exhaust filling the air caused distortions to the view of the highway and the bridge beyond. As dusk approached, lights came on, and the cityscape beyond the river began to glow with a life of its own. Ennopy watched the changing scene with disinterest, impatient to be downtown where he could continue his search for Steele and his family.

Traffic had slowed to a bumper-to-bumper crawl, and horns honked continuously as drivers lost their tempers in fits of road rage. Ennopy sat analyzing the traffic patterns, looking for a break, when his internal comsystems suddenly alerted him to an incoming message. Another biomek had been attacked yesterday, its central control section damaged. All other meks were thereby commanded to reorder their structures, relocating their control sections to a more protected part of their seven-piece anatomical groupings.

Ennopy considered as he watched the flow of traffic start up again. Relocating his control sections would mean morphing, something that would drain his meager reserves of energy and endanger his mission.

For the first time in his existence, he decided not to comply, a fact that was to affect his future in a very big way.

* * *

Angel and Cutter watched Stray and the police officers pull out of her driveway, then they strolled through the darkness back to her white Cherokee. Cutter glanced over at his woman, wondering what she was thinking. The events of the day had been unexpectedly

133

horrific, and he knew she must be upset about the death of her ex-boyfriend.

He said, "Angel, I'm sorry about—about Kowalski."

She turned to give him a look of disbelief. "How can you say that? What you did--what you almost did with your Will--was obscene."

Cutter looked startled by her accusation, then hurt. For a moment he didn't reply, then all at once he threw back his head and laughed.

"My sweet Angel. What could you possibly know about the true nature of obscenity?"

"I know that using your 'abilities' to make a man commit suicide is obscene." She replied quietly.

Suddenly he was angry. How dare she rebuke him? It was his natural instinct to use his Will, after all, but he'd fought against it because of his love for her. Yet she thought she knew obscenity when she saw it? He tore his shirt open, buttons popping and flying in every direction, revealing the ugly wound below his collarbone.

"*This* is obscene!" he shouted at her, his voice echoing off the surrounding trees. He waved a hand at the scars on his face. "This! This is obscene!" He closed his eyes in a pained wince and spun away from her, memories blasting upon his consciousness. "The greys' pogrom is obscene..."

Angel stopped walking, stunned by his outburst. Until now, he'd been so calm, that she'd thought that he'd been unmoved by the day's happenings. She said, "You're right. But the greys think your people are out of control. You couldn't allow your desire for revenge to prove them right." Then she spied something on his shirt, a stain that hadn't been there that morning. "Cutter! You're bleeding! Did—did Jeff cut you?"

He glanced down at his dirt- and soot-smudged shirt, and then pulled it away from his side where new dampness had stuck the fabric to his skin. He must have re-opened the wound when he'd ripped open his shirt. "Guess so," he said, his anger spent. Beneath his clothing was a long, thin cut where the scorched carving knife had grazed him.

Angel got the first aid kit out of her car. As she

began to clean out his wound under the SUV's dome light, she asked softly, "Why didn't you tell me about Jeff?"

"I couldn't. You cared about him. I thought it would hurt you too much to know what he was really like—what he was capable of." He paused as she put some peroxide on the cut. "I thought you'd think I was just jealous of him."

"Oh, Cutter." Angel grinned. "Sometimes you can be so—human." She dried his wound, covered it with antiseptic and gauze, and then began packing up the first aid kit.

He grinned back, his best arrogant grin. "Is that an insult or a compliment?"

"Take it any way you like it." She countered, and then nodded toward the tree line where the moon was just coming up over the tops of the trees. "Look. Isn't it beautiful?"

"Yes." He agreed, but he was staring at her.

Angel shivered under his pale gaze. "It's getting cold," she commented, but knew that it wasn't the temperature that had caused her to tremble.

He took her into his arms, and kissed her softly. She returned his kiss, said, "We'd better get on the road. We have to get home." But she lingered in his embrace.

"We will," was all he said.

Chapter 17: A Brief Interlude

The old man had spoken at great length, and by now it was only an hour or so before dawn. He'd just told me about the night he'd killed Jeff Kowalski, and Angel's reaction to the fight.

"She loved me even then." The old man said, his voice heavy with reminiscence. "Even knowing what I was capable of." He shuddered, and I wondered what thoughts were rushing through his mind that he wasn't voicing.

The moon had set while he'd spoken, throwing our surroundings into a pre-dawn blackness, except for the dim light from the lantern. In the ensuing silence, the constant drone of mosquitoes seemed magnified. I waited for "Al" to continue with his tale.

At long last, he said in a strained voice, "We made love beneath a full moon that night. A passionate coupling that will never be equaled by anyone, a joining of bodies and minds and souls." His voice was dry and grating now, unaccustomed to such extended use. He paused as another shudder ran through him. After a moment, he grabbed a stick of gnarled wood to use as a cane, and with a grunt of effort, pushed himself up from his chair to a standing position. "That's all for tonight, boy."

"What?" I wasn't sure I'd heard him correctly. Why was he terminating the interview?

"I said, 'That's all'." He repeated in his gravelly voice. "I'm tired, and I'm going to my shack." He began to hobble away from me, his gait awkward and unsteady.

"Wait!" I got to my feet, my limbs stiff from sitting too long. My action disturbed a cloud of mosquitoes, and they buzzed around my enviro-patch protected body.

"No," he said, "Come back tomorrow. You want the rest of your story; come back tomorrow."

He turned to glance back, shook his head, and continued toward his shanty. Even in the blackness, I could tell by his exaggerated movements that something was wrong. He took perhaps ten more steps, and then doubled over, leaning on his makeshift cane, and a groan escaped him.

I grabbed the lantern, and hurried to his side, trying not to trip on tussocks of swamp grass. "Al? What's wrong?"

The old man shook his head again. "Nothing that concerns you . . . I don't need your help, boy." Despite the words, his face registered his distress.

We were in the middle of nowhere, I had no clue as to what was wrong with him, and it didn't seem like the old bastard was going to cooperate. I said, "Al, tell me what's happening!"

"Final stages," he gasped as another wave of pain washed over him. "Even just thinking about her brings it on. Should've known better. Leave me, I'm alright!" He attempted to straighten, but the hand on his cane was shaking, his knuckles white.

I was about to protest, when my gaze met his. His pale eyes bored into mine, and he said in a voice that was suddenly strong enough to boom like thunder, "Go on, get out of here!"

I had no choice and no will. I took his lantern, and left him there, in the middle of the darkened swamp, alone. By the time I found my way back to my car, it was dawn.

* * *

Late the next day found me trudging reluctantly back through the snake and alligator infested swamp in search of "Al's" shack. It hadn't been easy to find the first time, and damn if it wasn't harder to find the second. I'd parked my car by the side of the road, reluctant to leave its air-conditioned interior, and had taken the over-grown path through the swamp grass and bushes, the high humidity and blazing sun reducing me to a wilted mess. By the time I found his shanty, on the edge of the murky pond, the sun was beginning to sink below the trees, and I had been just about ready to give up.

It appeared as if by magic, a rough-boarded shack with a tin roof and a small front porch, shaded by a few huge cypress trees. I mounted the pair of wooden steps, and knocked at the unpainted door. It opened at my touch, so I entered. The interior was suffocatingly hot, despite the shade from the trees, and depressingly dark.

137

My eyes traveled around the inside of the single room, noting the dark fabric curtains, the clean wooden floor, and tidy but sparse furnishings. In the bed against the far wall, the old man half sat, half reclined. He was so still, that for a long moment I again feared he was dead. His pale eyes were closed, and his mutilated hands seemed claw-like on top of the thin blanket. The heat was stifling, and my mind entertained thoughts of heat stroke, until I discerned the slight rise and fall of his bony chest.

I said, "Al?"

He jumped, his almost-white eyes flying open, and stared at me for a long moment before recognition settled in. "Oh," he said, "It's you."

He must have been lying there all day, in the oppressive heat. I looked around, and spying a well pump, I pumped a glassful, and brought him some water. He sipped tentatively, gratefully, and then said in a scratchy voice, "I didn't think you'd come back, boy. I'm glad you did. I want to finish what we started."

I said, "How are you feeling?"

He shrugged his thin shoulders, and looked away, and I could read the humiliation in his posture. "You weren't meant to witness that." He told me in a gruff manner.

"You shouldn't've sent me away." I chided gently. "What if you didn't make it back here?"

"I did, didn't I?" He countered, and this time his pale eyes met mine evenly. "I'm not done yet, boy, believe me."

And, after he'd recovered a bit, he continued with his story.

Chapter 18: Fallen Angels

Ellem Ennopy stood before the door to Stray's Upper East Side apartment, undecided. The operative was obviously not at home, and he could search the premises without being impeded. But to accomplish what he desired, he'd have to both enter and leave the man's domicile without being detected. He would be perfectly capable of achieving this goal, if he could morph one of his hands into a key. To do so, however, would also mean expending valuable energy, and according to his internal register, he had very little to spare, if he was to save enough for the actual mission. He hesitated a moment, then decided that the resultant energy loss would be worth it. Faster than thought, he sent a message to his lower left appendage. His left index finger elongated, inching its way into the first of the four keyholes, then spreading into the grooves and fissures inside. With a quick turn of his wrist, the first of the four dead bolt locks opened. Several moments later, he was in the apartment.

Every piece of expensive furniture, the placement of every object d'art, registered on Ennopy's senses and was recorded. When he left the place, everything would have to have been returned to its original position; nothing could appear to have been disturbed.

He moved with precision and speed. It was not long before he found what he was looking for, and was again on the road. His new goal was Philadelphia, Pennsylvania.

* * *

Angel yawned, coming down the stairs, Matrix in her arms. Cutter was already at the table in the small kitchen, downing some coffee and a bagel.

They had gotten in very late last night. After dealing with Jeff Kowalski's death and the state police, they had released their pent-up stress in unprecedented lovemaking beneath a full moon. She found it odd that she could even have considered such an action, after the gory events of the day. Yet, at the time, it had seemed so natural to consol each other in that manner. Cutter exuded a sexuality that she couldn't resist, and they'd both been feeling so much in need of each other's support, both mental and physical.

As she came into the kitchen with Matrix, Cutter looked up. "There's my boy!" Matrix had been asleep in bed, when they'd arrived home. They'd gone into his room and kissed him as he'd slept, before thanking Toni for babysitting, and saying good night.

"Dodden-dee!" exclaimed the child happily.

Angel stuttered. Matrix was only about three months old, and shouldn't be speaking words. "W-what did he say?" she gasped.

"Dodden-dee!" repeated the boy with enthusiasm. "Dodden-dee-dee!"

Cutter grinned, holding out his arms for the baby. "Matrix, hey! How are ya, Trickster?" he explained to Angel, "Dodden's our people's word for 'father'." He glanced at her as he took the boy, and saw the look on her dark features. "What?"

"Cutter, he's –he's only a baby! He shouldn't be able to talk yet!"

Steele's smile widened. "When's Mommo going to realize you're no ordinary baby, huh?" he said to Matrix. Then, to Angel he said, "I thought you would have expected this."

"Expected what? What's happening to him?"

Her voice shook, and he realized just how unnerved she was over their son's behavior. He said, "On the home world, things are vastly different. We're being wiped out at a much faster rate than we can reproduce. To compensate, our offspring gestate much more quickly, as you've seen with him."

Angel's eyebrow lifted. "—and?"

"For the first five years of life, our children mature at a pace three times faster than human offspring do, so that they're emotionally and sexually mature by the time they're five. It's necessary for our survival. Which is also the main reason for our breeding program on Earth. You know this."

"Yeah, but you never said anything about rapid development—"

"It's just our biology," he defended himself. "Why?

Does it pose a problem?"

Angel rolled her eyes. "How are we supposed to explain this accelerated growth rate to other people? You know--to doctors, or to teachers?" She sighed. "What are we supposed to do--keep moving from place to place until he's grown? I need my job—"

He didn't have an answer. To distract her, he said, "—Speaking of which, aren't you going to be late?"

She glanced at the kitchen clock. "Oh, my gosh! I've got to get out of here! What are you two going to do today?"

"Stray's picking us up. He and I have a meeting in the Northeast. We'll take The Trickster with us."

"Hmmmm--OK." Angel agreed, taking a quick sip of Cutter's coffee. She gave him and Matrix each a kiss, grabbed her purse and left, a feeling of disquiet going with her.

* * *

"The tracking devices are working perfectly. We're identifying meks all over the country."

The men of the resistance were gathered in a conference room in a hotel in Northeast Philadelphia. They sat at an oval table, bowls of pretzels and carafes of coffee breaking the smooth surface.

Cutter nodded, satisfied. Good. Then Ace hadn't died in vain. He said, "How's the new weapon coming along?"

On the floor by his feet, Matrix chewed on his key ring, getting drool all over the keys. He grinned at the sight, despite a feeling of weariness. He hadn't slept well last night, and had been up way before dawn after having experienced more nightmares. "--What?"

"I said, they're still working on it." Repeated Stray. "Ace's notes were incomplete, and the guys in the lab are having a little trouble. I'm sure they'll figure it out, though."

Steele nodded again. Ace's woman had turned his notes over to the resistance immediately following his death. But there were important gaps in the information, presumably things that were known only to Covington, and the operatives in the lab were having unanticipated

141

problems in developing a weapon that would stop the biomeks for good.

Matrix dropped the key chain, and lifted his arms. "Dodden?"

"Yeah, ok, buddy." Cutter picked him up, and addressed the other men in the room.

"Any other business that needs taking care of?" He wanted to get done here, and take his son home for a nap. Come to think of it, he could use a nap, himself. He stifled a yawn.

One of the older members of the resistance stood. He cleared his throat, and seemed to be hesitant to speak.

Steele said, "What have you got, Wink?"

The man shifted his gaze away, studying the rug. "One of our operative's woman is pregnant—"

Murmurs of approval went around the room.

"—It's not as easy as that," continued the man named Wink. "The operative was killed in the Palm Sunday Massacre, leaving his woman alone to have their unborn child—"

"We're all family. Any and all help we can give her, give her." Said Cutter evenly.

Still the man seemed disinclined to speak. He continued to avoid looking at Steele. "There's some reluctance on her part to have the child."

"What?" The very idea was ludicrous. "Is there a reason for this 'reluctance'?"

Wink cleared his throat again.

One of the other operatives grew impatient. "Wink? What is it you're trying to say?"

"She, the mother, has seen Matrix. She says she's afraid of giving birth to a—that is, to an abnormal child. She wants to abort."

The room broke out in immediate protests, and Stray motioned for silence.

In the ensuing stillness, Cutter shifted his son onto his bad leg and leaned forward in his chair. His jaw clenched and unclenched, and he spoke distinctly. "First of all, my boy is not 'abnormal'."

"No, of course not. I didn't mean to imply anything of the sort. But, to humans, your son seems rather—

different."

Cutter heaved a sigh. When two totally alien cultures collided, things like this were bound to happen. "I'll talk to her. We've got to preserve any future members of our species. Are any of the other women having doubts? Second thoughts?" So far, worldwide, 67 human women were pregnant with off-worlder children. No one mentioned any other misgivings, and he went on, "Is the woman here at this moment?"

Wink nodded. "She's outside."

Steele took up his cane and stood, holding his son in his other arm. "Alright. It's lunch time anyway, let's adjourn and I'll speak with her now."

Stray watched him leave the room with Matrix, his shuffling limp betraying his weariness, and then officially adjourned the meeting.

* * *

"Nancy?" Ace's pair bond! The woman who was asking for an abortion, was Ace's pair bonded mate! Matrix sat on his father's lap, now teething on the tracking device around Cutter's neck, as Steele exclaimed in shock at the woman who had just entered the hotel lobby.

"You didn't know? Wink didn't tell you it was me?"

"He said it was someone whose mate was killed on Palm Sunday..."

"I suppose he didn't want to implicate me, incase I changed my mind before you and I met."

"Why?" he questioned, without further preliminaries. "Nancy, its Ace's baby, why wouldn't you want it?" He stood, and they moved into a private alcove, Cutter's voice a quiet hiss. The place was decorated in 1970's colors and smelled of stale cigarettes.

"It's not that I don't want our baby, Cutter. I—I just don't feel like I can do this alone. It's something Ace and I wanted to do together—"

"Ace was one of my best friends. I understand. But, Angel didn't expect to have Matrix alone, either, and she did." He chose a seat on a divan, getting the baby settled on his lap, and Nancy joined them.

"I beg your pardon?" She stared at Matrix, still happily teething on Cutter's tracking device.

143

"When our son was born, I wasn't with her." He explained, and his features darkened as usual at the memory of his abduction by Ennopy. "The most important day of my life, and I wasn't there. The greys took that from me." His voice was heavy with anger and bitterness. He gulped, pushing those feelings down, and forced himself to lighten up. "But Ace was with her, right after Matrix was born. He gave Angel the support I couldn't. If there's anything I can do to help you with this, I'll do it. Just please don't end your baby's life."

Nancy's eyes burned with tears. "I'm so afraid, Cutter." She insisted in a whisper.

Again, Steele's emotions changed swiftly. "Because Matrix isn't 'normal'?" he asked sarcastically. He studied the top of his son's head, clenching his jaw to keep from saying anything he'd regret.

"Is that what Wink told you I said? No. It's just that, I'm not sure I can handle *any* baby, let alone one that's—that's, you know, alien."

He heaved a deep, weary sigh. "Nancy, I'm going to tell you the same thing I told Wink. We're all Family. We'll all do whatever it takes to help you."

"Even be there with me, when I'm in labor?" It was a demand, yet spoken in a timid voice.

A strange look crept over Cutter's face. He said, "I'll be there myself, if that's what you want. It would be the greatest honor, if I could do for you, what Ace did for my woman and me. I mean it."

The sincerity in his voice could not be mistaken, and Nancy nodded ever so slowly.

Comprehending, Cutter sighed again, this time with relief. He looked down at the baby in his arms. Matrix had fallen asleep at last.

* * *

Ellem Ennopy sat watching the row house. No one would be home yet. There were no cars in the alley behind the brick building, none in the garage. He'd checked. He sat, parked in his gray Nissan, in a space across the street, waiting. Watching.

He'd know when Steele arrived. The lights in the house would go on, and that's when Ennopy would make his move. For the second time that day, he checked his power supply. There should be just enough left for him to morph one last time before attaining his goal. It would take a much softer guise, for him to keep a baby from becoming alarmed. Especially one with the sensitivities of Steele's race. He'd already chosen a set of feminine features to wear. The face of a woman known to the resistance. It would get him into the house, and it would keep Steele's child pacified. He smiled.

And waited. And watched.

* * *

Cutter arrived home, Matrix still asleep in his arms. He entered the house through the basement door, as his friend's car drove off into the gathering dusk. As usual he was late. The meeting with Nancy had not held him up, but the reports that came in later had. Late that afternoon, the men in the labs had discovered the information missing from Ace's notes, and were now on the road to developing the weapon Covington had initially proposed. It looked like things were finally going to take a turn for the better.

The only fly in the ointment for Steele was the decision to use such a weapon. As the Earth-side resistance leader, it fell to him to make that decision. Until now, his people had passively resisted the grey's attempts to wipe them out. Once the weapon was fully developed, they would be able to destroy all of the biomeks, and possibly many greys along with them. Should they turn their resistance into an offensive war? Or would that prove that the greys had been right about them all along? Cutter struggled with the question as he unlocked the door to his home.

Angel's car was in the garage, and he called her name softly, as he carefully carried Matrix up the stairs to the first floor, his bad leg a little stiff. The basement steps led into the kitchen, and he opened the door to find the room empty, Angel's purse on the table. He proceeded through the dining room, and on into the living room where a light was lit in welcome, then stopped short.

The front door was slightly ajar.

"Angel?" he called again, louder this time. He

145

stepped through the door, and out onto the front stoop. The small front yard was empty, the street quiet. A few doors down, a neighbor waved. Cutter returned the gesture with the cane in his free arm, then carried his son back into the house, shutting the door behind him.

He took the baby upstairs, his heart beginning to hammer. A feeling of dread washed over him, but he pushed it down. Perhaps Angel was in the bathroom, or lying down, or—Or what?

Matrix never moved as Cutter placed him in his crib and covered him with his favorite blanket. He kissed the baby's forehead, and then left the room, closing the door behind him.

"Angel?" There was a note of panic in his voice now, as he searched the bathroom, and finally, their bedroom. Angel was not in either of those places.

Steele gulped, then took a deep breath, exhaled, and began to go through the rooms again. Perhaps she'd left a note.

Where would she go on foot? his mind demanded.

The phone rang, and he descended the stairs as quickly as he could, eager to hear her voice on the other end of the line.

"Hello?"

"Cutter?"

Steele's heart dropped. "Stray. Angel's gone—"

"What?"

"She's gone. Her car and purse are here, but she's not home—"

"Are you sure? Have you looked everywhere?"

"Of course I'm sure. Look, the front door was open, when I got home—"

"Calm down, there's got to be a reason—"

"You calm down! I'm telling you, she's gone! I think the greys got her—"

"They greys don't use doors, Cutter, you know that." Stray's voice was patient and soothing. He said, "Where's Matrix?"

"I just put him to bed, but—"

"Ok, look. Call Toni. Have her come over to watch Matrix, and you and I'll go look for Angel. I'm on the cell phone in my car." Stray had been heading back to his apartment in NY. "I'm turning around, it'll only take me about 45 minutes to get to your place, OK? You listening?"

"Yes, but—"

"Just sit tight. I'll be there as soon as I can." And the other end of the line went dead.

Steele just stared at the phone in his hand, his feeling of dread growing once more. It wasn't until he'd hung up the phone, that he looked down and noticed that the small indicator light on his tracking device was lit.

* * *

Angel came-to lying on a flat surface, an invisible cushion of air holding her pinned down. The brilliant glare off the smooth white walls gave her an immediate headache, and she closed her eyes, trying to figure out where she was. The last thing she remembered was answering a knock at her front door.

She frowned, trying to think past the throbbing in her head. Who had been at the door? A vague feeling of uneasiness came over her as she tried to recall what had happened.

She opened her eyes again, and gazed around, stunned as she recognized the seamless, arched ceiling, and curved walls of the interior of a grey's examination room. Her heart began to hammer with dread, and her hands grew cold as anxiety welled up within her, pushing aside all efforts to remember her recent past.

She was with the greys again!

How had she gotten here? She didn't remember being visited by any little grey men, and she certainly hadn't come here on her own. In fact, she'd been waiting for Cutter to get home with Matrix, when Toni had arrived —

And then memory came flooding back. Her first encounter with what she could only guess had been a biomek.

It had still been light, when she'd pulled her Cherokee into the garage and parked. She'd closed the garage door, and entering the door to the house, had gone upstairs into the kitchen where she'd put her purse on the table. She'd gone through the dining room and into the

147

living room, where she'd lit a lamp, and had then gone upstairs to change.

She'd just come back downstairs, when there was a knock at the front door.

She opened it, to find Toni Russo on the front stoop.

"Toni!" she'd exclaimed. "What're you doing here? How've you b—"

She cut herself short. Although the person in her doorway looked very much like Toni Russo, it was not. There was a cold calculation in the woman's eyes that was unlike anything Angel had ever seen. She backed away a step, a shiver running down her spine. The woman advanced through the doorway, and into the house.

"Who are you?" demanded Angel.

For answer, the simulacrum grabbed her by the arm, and dragged her further into the living room, growling in a deep masculine voice, "Where is the child?"

Angel fought and struggled against a grip of astonishing power, but to no avail. "What do you want?" She asked, her mind racing. She had no tracking device. No one had expected that anyone, other than the off-world operatives, would need one. But at that moment, Angel found herself wanting something to confirm her sudden suspicions that this was indeed a biomek.

"Where's the child?" repeated the woman in the same deep voice.

Angel decided to try evasion. "What do you want with my son?"

The biomek had swung its free arm in a wide arc, connecting with Angel's chin and knocking her senseless. Angel had felt her grip on reality loosen, and had lost consciousness before she hit the floor.

Now, as her memories returned, she became aware of the danger she was in. Thoughts of what the biomek had done to her mate turned her blood to ice water. The greys wanted Matrix. What would they do to her, in order to get him? Here, in the domain of the greys, any horror she could imagine was possible, and in her present circumstances, she was totally at their mercy. If they had any.

At that very moment, three of the grey aliens materialized.

* * *

"How would this work again?" Cutter found it difficult to concentrate on what the operative was saying, most of his attention focused on worrying about Angel. Once he'd gotten over the initial shock and panic of her abduction, he'd become silent and brooding. The indicator light on his tracking device had been lit, warning him that a biomek was in, or had recently been in, his row home. By the time Stray had arrived, Cutter had been over the entire place with a fine-tooth comb, looking for clues, but without luck. He still had no idea as to who the mek intruder was, or where it had taken Angel.

He'd met the young newcomer operative at a local deli, and they'd walked to the nearby park to talk, Matrix asleep in a stroller. They chose a park bench under a large oak tree and sat.

The operative was a young man named Diver, with thick brown hair and a trim build. He was a scientific genius who had been sent to replace Ace, and who had uncovered the missing information in Covington's notes. He sighed with all the impatience of youth, and said to Cutter, "As I told you before, the meks are basically clusters of seven matter/energy transposers. Each single transposer unit has the ability to turn its own limited amount of matter into energy, and the energy back into matter. But they can't use this energy as fuel, because that would be consuming their own resources, so the entire cluster runs off a battery-sized micro reactor. In each cluster, one unit is designated as the central control section. This section gives orders to the entire cluster, much the way our brains control our bodies."

Cutter frowned. "I understand all of that, boy! What's your point?"

Diver glowered back, and continued, "Ok. Bear with me. A biomek cluster is composed of these units, each unit being comprised of a certain amount of matter. This matter cannot be added to, or detracted from. When a mek morphs, and transposes this matter into energy, the same is true: no energy is added or detracted. If it morphs into

149

a shape of decreased matter, the extraneous energy is then stored in the central control cluster until needed. You follow me?" Cutter nodded. "Good. Ok, what if extra matter were introduced into the central control unit?"

Cutter shrugged as a stiff breeze stirred the leaves of the tree they were sitting under. "There'd be an imbalance."

Diver grinned. "Right. And Ace's theory is that this imbalance would result in a chain reaction causing total destruction of the entire cluster. Now. How do we introduce this extra matter? What kind of matter do we introduce? A bullet?"

"No." said Cutter. "We've tried that. A bullet momentarily disintegrates the mek, but it just re-integrates itself by morphing."

"Exactly. Projectiles pass through the mek's matter without resultant damage, because it morphs the injury away. Even if it's blown apart by a blast, it can reintegrate itself. It's got a kind of super elasticity. However, if we were to inject a small amount of heavy water into the central core using say, a needle or a dart, this would be enough to cause an imbalance and a chain reaction."

"Why heavy water?"

"We think the deuterium would react with the energy stored in the control unit."

Cutter nodded, studying the fountain beyond their bench. "What kind of reaction are we talking about?"

"Let's just say, you wouldn't want to be in the immediate area."

"And you're telling me we have the ability to deliver such darts without risking the lives of our own people?"

Diver's grin widened as he held up what appeared to be a blowgun. "Simplicity is sometimes best."

Cutter nodded again. So. This was *It*. They had a way to theoretically destroy the meks. The only question was, should they? Or would wiping out another biological life form, albeit a manufactured one, prove that they were as bad as the greys?

He said, "Does Stray have all of this information?" he stood, and Diver followed suit.

"Not yet."

"Ok. See that he gets it. Have the weapons made and distributed to the resistance groups. But do not, under any circumstances, hand them out to the individual operatives, unless under direct orders from me. Is that clear?"

Diver looked disappointed. "We have the opportunity here to—"

"I know what we can do, boy!" thundered Cutter. "But not unless I order it. Is that perfectly clear?"

Diver nodded, chastised, and Cutter dismissed him, his thoughts racing.

He had to be absolutely certain who held Angel, before he started an offensive that would wipe out the biomeks indiscriminately. If they destroyed her abductor before they knew her location, she could be lost to him forever.

With that thought, the sun clouded over.

* * *

Two weeks later

"Stop the film there. See?"

Stray pointed to the screen, showing a large, blond man with a beard entering his apartment. He and Cutter were in Stray's living room, viewing a home security cam's recording of the day Angel had been abducted.

"Ennopy!" Cutter's voice cracked as he spat out the name.

Stray nodded. "Uh-huh. And look. Watch this." He hit the play button, and the video resumed, showing the biomek from another angle, just inside Stray's home. He'd had security cameras hidden in various places throughout his domicile, and the biomek had been totally unaware that his intrusion had not gone undetected. As the film rolled, Ennopy was seen to pick something up from Stray's desk, and study it. Stray paused the recorder again, and it was suddenly clear that the mek was looking at a photo.

The interrupted film was grainy, but the photo Ennopy held in his hand was visible enough. It was a picture of Angel, Cutter, Toni Russo and Matrix.

Cutter found himself unable to speak for a moment, remembering the day the picture had been taken. Toni had joined them for dinner, to celebrate Angel's birthday,

151

and—

He inhaled sharply, startling Stray.

"What?"

"It was Ennopy! Ennopy abducted Angel. And that's how he must have gotten into our house!" He exclaimed.

"What?" said Stray again.

"He posed as Toni! Angel wouldn't think twice about letting Toni in."

Stray's head bobbed in agreement. Then a thought occurred to him.

"Ennopy has copied Toni's features. He's made her as an operative—"

"—Which means she's in danger." Finished Cutter. And Matrix was with Toni, at her home! His eyes widened. "And so is my son!"

"We've got to get Toni out of town—" began Stay, following the same train of thought.

"I've got to get Matrix!" began Cutter at the same time. "Better yet," he continued, "I'll call and have Toni come here." They were at Stray's expensive, three floor apartment in New York. He and Matrix hadn't gone back to the house since Angel's abduction. Now that the biomek knew where they were, they had to keep moving again. He fumbled for his cell phone; the one Angel had given him only recently, to keep him in constant contact.

When Toni arrived, they hurriedly explained the reason they'd called her. Cutter kissed his son, grateful that nothing had happened to him or Toni, and then set him on the floor to play.

Matrix chewed on Cutter's ring of keys, then began to cry.

"I think his teeth are bothering him." Said Toni helpfully. He'd been teething almost constantly for the past several weeks.

"Mommo!" wailed the baby. "Mommo-me-me!"

"Yeah, I know, Buddy," said Cutter, picking his son back up. "I miss Mommo, too—Oh!" All at once, he doubled over, Toni grabbing Matrix as he did. He groaned, clenching his teeth tightly together, his features pulling into a grimace.

Stray was beside him instantly. "Cutter?"

His friend didn't speak, holding his midsection and rocking back and forth on the chair, unable to even breathe, his features pale.

Stray said, "Is it the Withering?"

Cutter nodded wordlessly, still enduring the spasm. When at last it passed, and he was able to draw a breath, he said tightly, "It's started again . . . I'll be ok in a minute . . . "

Toni looked shaken. "What's started? What's wrong with you, Cutter?"

"I'm going through a kind of hormonal withdraw." He explained. "Don't worry about it. Take Matrix upstairs, and put him to bed for me, will you?"

Toni nodded. Cutter kissed his son, and she took Matrix upstairs to give him a bath before putting him to bed.

When she had gone, Stray asked, "Are you sure you're alright?" Like all the rest of their people, he knew how bad the beginning stages of the Withering were supposed to be.

Cutter nodded, but his face was still pasty, and his hands shook. He clasped them to hide the tremors and swallowed, changing the subject, "Has there been any word on Ennopy's location?" If they could find the biomek who had abducted Angel, they would be halfway to finding her.

Stray shook his head. Word was out that they were looking for Ennopy, but the mek seemed to have disappeared off the face of the Earth. He was about to speak, when his own cell phone rang. He answered it, spoke a few words, then put the phone back into his brief case, his face stricken.

Cutter took one look at his friend, and knew that the news was bad. He said, "Is it—Angel?"

Stray nodded. "Cutter—"

"Tell me, Stray." He said, his chest tight with tension. "Just say it."

"That was Diver. They picked up a human contact who'd been recently abducted—"

"And?"

"He claims he saw Angel aboard the greys' ship. He says—he says they—killed her. We've—had several confirmations."

Cutter's face drained. He started to speak, then doubled up again. He rode the waves of pain silently, focused only on his tremendous loss. This time when the attack passed, he straightened, his features hard, his pale blue eyes cold and distant. He managed to say, in a level voice, "Have them distribute the new weapons, Stray."

"The blow guns?" Had Steele at last decided to annihilate the biomeks?

"Yes." He said harshly. The meks had killed his woman. "Wipe the bastards out. Wipe them ALL out."

Chapter 19: Final Stages

The old man finished speaking, his words cut off with a sharp gasp. I told him that perhaps it would be better if we conducted this interview from a hospital room.

"You sound as if you need medical attention."

"Medical attention?" he jeered. "No, not the way you think of it ... I'm in the last stages... not much your hospitals could do ... "

"Last stages?"

"Don't worry . . . I've timed this very carefully . . . I should have just enough . . . strength left . . . you'll get the rest of your story, boy."

"That's not what I'm concerned about!" I protested, and then went on. "You're obviously ill." I glanced around the mean little shack, wondering how he'd even managed to survive so far. "You don't have any visible means of financial support, how have you continued to live here without food and electricity?"

Al scoffed. "Look around, boy! You just pumped me a glass of water. There's a well. Got an outhouse out back. Sometimes Stray or Nancy sends a courier with food and lamp oil. Humph! Food," he mused. "Not that I need food. There's an orange grove on the other side of the swamp, and this place is a smorgasbord of insects." He glanced up at me, his blue eyes betraying a hint of amusement. "Ever try raw Palmetto bugs?"

I almost gagged at the thought of eating a cockroach, but managed to choke down the urge, surprised at his levity. "NO!" I said.

Al chuckled, and then suddenly went into another fit. When the attack had passed, he looked even worse than he had before. He said, "Perhaps. . . we could take another small break."

I nodded. "I'm overdue at work, and need to contact my boss, anyway." And I went outside to use my cell phone.

The sun had dipped closer to the horizon, and the day's heat was at last giving way to a cooler breeze as the wind shifted and blew in off the ocean. I dialed my editor's number. I dreaded speaking with the she-dragon. She was still at her desk, (of course, what else had I expected from a workaholic?) and answered her phone.

"Laura Woodhouse."

I announced myself and proceeded to tell her why I hadn't concluded the interview yet, ending with, "I don't know. If the old geezer's telling the truth, he might be dying. Maybe you should get down here and judge the validity of his story for yourself."

I expected an argument. Instead she said, "Fine. I'll be there later tonight." And then she hung up.

I replaced the phone, and went inside the suffocatingly hot shack to hear more of the Old man's tale.

Chapter 20: Shallow Victories

When the greys in the lab allowed all seven of Ellem Ennopy's transposer-units to reintegrate, he came back to consciousness aware of several changes within himself. As a precaution, a shielding mechanism had been installed, to protect his body-cluster from harm in battle. As a reward for capturing and delivering Angel French, he'd also been fitted with another power pack. This one was a newer model, permanent and self-renewing. The third change was more insidious. They had implanted a neural device designed to transfer the grey's thoughts directly into his central control unit for translation and oral delivery to the Earth-side resistance movement.

Initially, the device was confusing to Ennopy. It put thoughts into his head that were not his. When he finally learned to distinguish the grey's thoughts from his own, he was ready to be used as a translator.

Thought of Angel caused his central control unit to automatically replay for him the event of her capture as it had occurred, his cybernetic version of memory.

He'd already morphed into the guise of a woman. He'd seen her face in a photo with Steel, which he'd found in Stray's apartment. The woman was known, then, not only to Steel and his family, but to the resistance as well.

He'd gone to the door of Steel's home and knocked. Cutter's woman had answered, recognizing his disguise as someone she called 'Toni'. He'd pushed past her, into the house, demanding the child. The woman had tried to dissuade him from his goal, and he'd had to silence her. He'd searched the place, only to find that Steele and the child were not there. By then, he'd realized that his available power was too low to continue his mission. There was no time to wait for Steele's arrival. He would have to abduct the woman instead of her child. He'd communicated his situation, requesting extraction, secured his captive, and had gone into hibernation mode.

His actions had acquired for him a new lease on life.

* * *

"I don't understand it," said Stray. "All the reports we're getting in, say that the new weapons aren't working. They're having no effect at all."

He and Cutter were sitting in a small diner at the cross roads of a major highway, the traffic outside a constant hum. A waitress came by and refilled their coffee cups, giving each of the men an appreciative glance. She was in her early thirties, with a woman's curves, a pleasant disposition and an easy grin. Stray followed her with his eyes, as she left.

Cutter noticed his friend's gaze, and said, "You should go for it. I mean, you've been down here how many years, and haven't bonded?" He sat, slouched at the table, his crossed arms resting on its edge; his jeans and tee shirt slightly rumpled from wear. The thought of Stray bonding only served to emphasize Angel's death, and tore at Cutter. His pale eyes involuntarily misted, and he looked quickly away.

Stray returned his attention to the table, and took a sip of his coffee. "That's not part of my mission parameters." He stated flatly, knowing what his friend must be feeling. In contrast, his own posture was erect and formal, his neutral colored suit perfectly pressed.

Steele's eyebrows shot upwards. "It's not?" According to his information, all the operatives who had gone Earth-side had been sent to accomplish the breeding program. This new knowledge surprised him, and turned his attention away from self-pity.

Stray smirked. "The home world authorities wanted at least a few of us down here that are thinking with this part of our anatomy." He indicated his skull.

There was a lot of sense in Stray's comment. Cutter was quiet for a moment, thinking. At last he said, "Then, why would they allow me to become—"

"You're a natural leader. You're passionate. Intuitive. The rest of our operatives follow you without question. I'm only here to rein in those passions, if necessary."

The other rolled his eyes and blew out his breath in disgust. "Then I'm a puppet!" Perhaps the authorities had been pulling his strings all along. Sending him the right people, and the right missions at just the right times.

"No, you're not. You've made all the decisions so far, haven't you?"

"Stray, just what are your orders?"

"I'm only to act, if I find that your reasoning has become--clouded."

"And has it?" He knew that the only reason he hadn't moved against the biomeks immediately was due to the fact that they had held Angel.

Stray sighed and looked away. *Was* Cutter's judgment impaired? He said, "I think you've been walking a fine line lately." And his gaze came back to meet Cutter's squarely.

Steele nodded. "At least you're honest." He shifted his focus to stare out the window, at the pedestrians on the street. Had he been performing his duties with any modicum of honesty? Or had he been thinking with his—

All at once, he sat bolt upright, almost spilling his coffee. Stray looked at him questioningly.

"Where's a biomek's brain located?" Cutter demanded.

"Huh?" the change of subject left Stray confused. "What are you talking about?"

"The meks. We've been targeting their brains, their control centers. But reports say our weapons haven't been successful. I don't think Ace's weapon is faulty, do you?"

"No, but you've lost me. What do you mean?"

"Maybe we've been targeting the wrong transposer units!" Steele exclaimed. "We've always assumed that the greys followed natural biology, when they designed the meks. What if they didn't? What if the control sections are located some place other than in the mek's heads?"

Stray grinned. "That, my friend, is why you are our leader." He stood, tossing some money onto the table. "Come on, let's go discuss this with Diver."

Cutter rose, grabbing his cane, and no longer feeling like such a puppet.

* * *

Cutter sat at the dining room table in Nancy Covington's home, surrounded by operatives. The table was opened out to its largest size, to accommodate the crowd, and they sat in thickly padded chairs with castors. Nancy was a professional SF novelist, and her home was large and expensive, with many rooms, and furnished with ultra modern furniture in neutral colors. Obviously with child, Nancy was serving them refreshments as they discussed the latest reports on the offensive against the biomeks.

Two months had passed since they had realized the reason for their weapon's ineffectiveness, and had corrected their strategy. Through trial and error, they had detected the location of the biomek's central control units, now located in the chest area, and had been enjoying an unprecedented success in destroying the cyborgs.

True to Diver's prediction, the weapons had caused dangerous chain reactions in the biomek's systems. Cutter knew first hand how powerful they were. Grieving over Angel's death, he'd risked himself, despite objections by Stray and the other resistance members, insisting on being the first to try the new weapons. In the very first targeting mission, he'd lost two fingers on his one hand, and several innocent by-standers had been killed, when the reaction occurred. None of them had expected an explosion of such tremendous force. The news media had called it a terrorist bombing. The resistance knew better. They were trying to wipe out the real terrorists.

The tide of the battle was turning at last, and the men of the resistance had gotten together to discuss recent results, and possible victory.

Diver said, "We are definitely winning. The greys can't manufacture enough biomeks to make up for their losses. We're destroying them, all across the world."

Enthusiastic cheers broke out, greeting the optimistic news.

"Ennopy hasn't been taken out, yet." Cutter reminded the men at the table. The blond cyborg had been targeted twice, without success, and none of the new reports ever mentioned the biomek's present location. He wondered why the hits had been ineffective. "Nor has the mek who killed Ace. I want them both destroyed. Until then, we haven't won."

The atmosphere dulled somewhat, the resentment

plain on a few faces.

Someone said, "You've been driving us all too hard. Give us a break. We ought to be celebrating."

Wink agreed, "Cutter, you're turning this into an attempt to exact personal revenge."

Steele's jaw set. Nancy Covington was nearly ready to deliver Ace's child alone, due to the Enemy's biomeks. Toni Russo sat playing with Matrix, in the next room. Now that she had been identified as a resistance sympathizer, her longish hair had been cut short and dyed auburn to disguise her looks. He listened to her prattle as she cared for his son, his mind seething with resentment against those who had killed his woman. Against the men who didn't want to pursue them. He didn't intend to give up the fight, until all of the grey's biomachines had been destroyed.

He said tightly, "Think what you want. I'm not quitting until we've annihilated every last one of those— bastards." His gaze wandered the faces at the table, waiting for Stray's objection. He was the watchdog, wasn't he? The one who would leash Cutter's violence, if he felt it was unwarranted.

It was then, that he noted Stray's absence. He had been so busy with the meeting; he hadn't realized that his friend was missing. "Where's Stray?"

There was an uncomfortable silence around the room.

Toni spoke up from the doorway, holding a yawning Matrix. "I'm going to put him down for his nap, now." Cutter nodded, giving his son an absent kiss and dismissing the interruption, then turned back to the men, insisting on an answer.

"Where's Stray?"

Wink cleared his throat. "Cutter—" he faltered, and then stopped.

Diver spoke up, his young face burning. Everyone knew, except Steele. "He was called to another meeting—"

"What do you mean, 'another meeting'?"

"You've gotten a little out of control." Said an older operative. "This obsession with destroying the mek who abducted your mate is affecting your judgment."

161

Another said, "We understand your need to avenge your woman, but—"

"You understand *NOTHING!*" thundered Cutter, slamming his fists down onto the table. There was an immediate silence, and knowing glances were exchanged between the men. Steele blew out his breath, and rolled his chair back with a push, turning away in disgust.

"The home world leaders wanted to discuss our recent activities with Stray." Informed the man next to Wink. "To assure themselves that you haven't been acting improperly."

Cutter turned back and eyed them all levelly. "You're not happy with the success we've had? You think I'm acting improperly? All right, then, I'll step down. But I won't stop trying to wipe—"

He caught his breath, and held it, fighting an attack of cramps. He hadn't been bothered all morning, so the onslaught took him off guard. When it had passed, he said, "Consider me resigned." He grabbed his cane, pushing himself up, and turned to leave the room, amid shouts of protest.

On his way out, Nancy Covington caught his arm. Her face was pale, and her eyes held a look of fear. "Cutter--!"

He stopped, caught by her urgency. "What's the matter, Nancy?"

"You promised . . . It's time.. ."

For a brief moment, he had no idea what she was talking about. Then it struck him.

"It's time? Oh, Nancy!" He turned and shouted for Toni. Nancy was about to give birth.

* * *

It had been a long day. Nancy's house was full to capacity with resistance members, all of the many bedrooms occupied. The pull-out couch in Nancy's living room was made up with sheets and blankets, too, and Cutter sat on top of them, his head in his hands, wearily going over the events of the day. The men had refused to accept his resignation, Nancy had given birth to a baby girl, and Stray still had not turned up.

Cutter rubbed at the back of his neck, sighing.

There were things he wanted to discuss. The doubts about himself that had been raised at today's meeting plagued him, gnawing away at his self-confidence, and underscoring the absence of Angel. He missed her so much; it hurt him to even think of her. He couldn't believe she was really dead. He needed to talk to a friend. He needed to talk to Stray.

Tony came back from putting Matrix to bed for the night. "Cutter, you should rest, too." She could see the exhaustion on his face. And the grief.

"I don't have time." He growled, covering the devastation he'd been feeling. "There's too much to do. When Stray gets here, send him to me immediately." And he got up and began to pace.

* * *

"The authorities were concerned that you've been advancing your personal vendetta. But I spoke on your behalf, and now they're satisfied." Stray grinned. Then his face hardened. "I just got word that the rest of the biomeks have been destroyed. The Greys want to talk terms. Our people agree."

"Do our authorities actually want to accept a surrender? Or do they want us to finish this once and for all?"

"It's up to you."

Cutter sighed deeply. This was his opportunity to prove that his people were better than the greys. Better than what the greys thought of them. He thought for a long moment. What would be better for his people? To destroy their enemy, or to show that they had mercy? He made a decision. "They trust me to set terms?"

"Yes. But I think you should know: The greys are sending Ennopy."

A change came over Steele's face. "Then this is our chance to take him out." The tone of his voice said he'd suddenly changed his mind entirely. "Where is this 'surrender' supposed to take place?"

"Somewhere remote, of course." Informed Stray, immediately accepting his leader's new decision. "Upon their insistence, there will be a delegation of greys present. They suggested Angel's property."

163

Steele's heart constricted, but his face registered nothing. Perhaps it would be a fitting place to destroy Ennopy. The very place where the biomek had nearly destroyed him. "Fine."

"I'll get some weapons togeth-" began Stray.

"--No." Cutter interrupted. Ennopy was one dangerous and wary character, as he well knew. The hit would have to be up close. Dangerously close. "This requires someone--expendable."

"*None* of our people are expend-"

"--I am. Without Angel, I'm nothing. I'll go." He paused as another intensely painful sensation washed over him. The spasms were getting closer together again, and he knew that the second stage of his withering would be commencing soon.

Stray waited for it to subside, before he said, "What about Matrix-? You can't just go and leave him without a mother or a father."

The reminder hurt, but Cutter barked out a sarcastic laugh. "I'm--no good to him anymore. Not like this. I'm dying. He's a survivor. He'll be ok, with you to teach him." He paused, letting the implication of his words register on his friend. Then he went on, thrusting his Will at the other man. "You know I've got to finish this, Stray. They killed my woman; I deserve my revenge."

Stray's Will met his. At first neither gave in, but Stray could feel his friend's greater power, and knew that if it came down to it, Steele's Will would prevail. He backed down and said, "You're our leader. We need you--"

"Come on, Stray. If Fox weren't dead, I'm sure I never even would have been picked to lead the Resistance. *He* would've—"

"You're wrong," interrupted Stray. "Fox was too brash. Our authorities knew that. That's why we needed *you*. That's why we still do."

"You'd make a far better leader, Stray. Even better than Fox would have. I've always known that. You're—" he searched for the right word, "—stable. And I don't want to shrivel up and die, anyway. I want to go out fighting. Let my end be worth something."

"Cutter, in your condition you might not be able to--"

"We're talking about Ennopy here, Stray. Don't worry about me, I'll complete the mission."

* * *

It was midmorning when Cutter and Stray arrived at Angel's property in the mountains. Matrix was asleep in a car seat in the back of the Jaguar. That Cutter had insisted on bringing his son on such a dangerous mission had puzzled Stray.

"Why don't you ask Toni to watch him? Or Nancy? Either of them would."

But Steele had been adamant. "I'm not leaving him with anyone. I want him to be present when I avenge his Mother's death."

"You're not thinking clearly, Cutter! Listen to yourself! I won't do it."

Steele had turned to Stray, his almost white eyes hard. "Don't make me use my Will against you, my friend. You know I'd win. Just do this for me. One last favor."

Against his better judgment, Stray had relented.

The sun was shining, the trees in their full summer foliage, and the area around the burned out cabin was lush with new growth. Cutter gave his son a kiss, his throat tight. If things went the way he'd planned, he wouldn't be coming back. He whispered, "I love you, Trickster." And got out of the Jaguar, ready to meet his destiny.

He walked the long distance up the rutted dirt driveway, memories blasting on his consciousness. He shook them off, preparing himself for the confrontation to come. Focusing on the present.

Something beyond the trees glowed brightly in the morning light, and Steele knew it was one of the greys' ugly squat ships. So. They were already here. His eyes traveled to the burnt-out ruin of Angel's cabin, and saw a man step out from around the remaining corner of the house, where the tree shadows were deepest. Ennopy.

Ennopy grinned, recognizing Steele. "They sent *you*? The leader of their resistance efforts? We're honored."

"'We'?" Cutter glanced past Ennopy, to the shadowed corner, saw movement in the surrounding clump of trees.

Ennopy said, "You, of all people, should know that we biomeks are a cooperative cluster. What you might not know is that my particular central control persona has been linked to that of the Greys' leader so that we may better communicate our demand for terms. I speak for them, now."

"We both know there'll *be* no 'terms'." said Cutter harshly. Concealed in his sleeve, was a hollow dart with just enough heavy water, to cause the biomek's destruction. Again, his mind wondered why Ennopy hadn't been affected by the previous attempts to destroy him.

Ennopy grinned. His masters had not lacked foresight. "'No terms'? Where's your compassion? Your forgiveness?" The biomek mocked. "We can force you to negotiate." Then he motioned, and the shadow behind him came into the light. A handcuffed human, surrounded by a number of armed greys.

Cutter froze, stunned, as he recognized the figure.

Angel!

Alive!

Angel was *alive!* His heart pounded heavily. This changed everything.

Every fiber of his being tingled. Every instinct cried out to him, to throw his Will at her, to compel her to him. An intense urge to mate with her, and renew their bond, overwhelmed his thoughts. He struggled to push it down. It took every ounce of his self-control not to follow those instincts, to remain where he was, not to gaze into her eyes. He knew a mek's capabilities. If she moved even an inch, Ennopy could finish her where she stood.

The tingling increased. Then the effects of the Withering slammed into him with such unexpected force that he gasped aloud. His gut suddenly constricted with severe pain, and his hands automatically balled into fists as he tried to bear it. He grunted in surprise, but his eyes never left the beautiful woman by Ennopy's side. Angel! He spoke over his suffering, his voice as steady as he could make it.

"You don't need my woman." He winced, gasping. "Let her go."

Ennopy grinned again. He watched Steele's reaction

with dispassionate interest. He'd seen him in the throes of withdraw before. He knew the symptoms, and recognized them now, but noted that they were stronger in the presence of the woman. "You're right. We don't need this one. We want your *son*, Cutter Steele. Give us your son, and you'll never have to see us again."

"*NO!*" The spasms receded, and his voice bellowed his refusal.

Cutter felt his anger and hatred boiling up within him, overriding even the residual sensations of the Withering. He hated the greys so much. It enraged him, that they could trap him this way. He couldn't act, with Angel in their midst, yet if he didn't, they'd seize the advantage. All it would take, would be one quick injection, and Ennopy would go down, and hopefully the greys with him. He *had* to make his move; it was the only way to finish this. He dropped the dart into his hand. *Do it,* he told himself, his muscles tensing.

Yet still he hesitated, his heart torn. Angel was alive! But she was too close. If he took out Ennopy, he might take her out, as well. Her presence was costing him control of the situation.

Do it, his inner voice urged again.

Ennopy saw his hesitation and said, "Then, give us your son, or I'll *kill* this woman."

With a feral growl, Cutter launched himself at the biomek, his arm poised, dart in hand. He sank it deep into the biomek's chest cavity, the place that they'd discovered held the biomek's control center.

Ennopy stepped back, startled, and activated his protective shielding. Cutter regained his balance, his eyes going wide at the tell-tale hum. The greys had never shielded their meks before. He hadn't expected the invisible energy field. He wouldn't get a second chance, now. He recovered from the jab, amazed that the mek hadn't gone down, and knowing that he'd just lost, not only his chance for revenge, but control of the situation as well. A small army of greys came out of the woods, all of them armed with their ray weapons, and surrounded the burned clearing.

Ennopy picked the dart out of his chest and threw

it to the ground. This was the way the resistance had destroyed all of the others of his kind. He laughed. "You need updated information." He said, with obvious enjoyment. "*My* control center was never located there."

Ennopy had the advantage now, and knew it, surrounded by his army of grey-skinned masters. But the greys still wanted Matrix. They spoke through Ennopy again: "We were willing to negotiate, and this assassination attempt on our biomek is how you repay our trust? With hatred?" Around him, the watching greys stirred, hands on their weapons.

"Willing to negotiate?" echoed Steele in an incredulous voice. "You showed up with an *army*! You can't blame us for defending ourselves, for attempting an attack!"

"Yet, you hesitated in your attack, despite your hatred of us, because you wanted to save this female. That shows us your species might have potential. Perhaps we'll give you another chance. Give us your boy, and we'll spare the rest of your race from our retaliation. Don't give him to us, and we'll annihilate all of you, starting with your woman. It's your choice."

Cutter Steele froze. The tables had turned, and there wasn't much he could do to remedy the situation.

"Ask anything else of me," Cutter spoke in a hoarse, anguished whisper. What new kind of psychological game was this? How could they make him choose between Angel and Matrix? Between the survival of his race, and his son?

Steele had been trained to put the continued existence of his people above all other considerations. If he surrendered his son, he could save his race from extinction at the hands of the greys, and maybe save Angel as well.

He knew what he had to do. Knew he was strong enough to do it, but was he strong enough to live with himself afterwards? He gathered himself, and glanced briefly at Angel, his features betraying his resolve.

Angel could see the light of cold, hard decision in his expression, even from across the clearing. She groaned and then slumped against the nearest tree, crying bitterly. "No, Cutter, *NO*... Not my baby..."

He pulled out his cell phone and punched the button for Stray's car number. When the other answered, he said calmly, "We've . . . negotiated after all. Bring my son to me."

* * *

Stray walked slowly up the driveway with Matrix, a puzzled look on his face. The sun was high now, and the shadows over them were deep and cool as he carried Steele's son up the rutted drive. The explosion he'd been waiting for had never come. Instead, Steele had 'negotiated' with the Enemy. When he was within earshot of Cutter, he said, "What's going on?"

Steele nodded toward the trees, and Stray's eyes grew large at the sight of Angel, alive and surrounded by so many armed greys.

Cutter said evenly, "It's an exchange: Matrix for our people. Including Angel."

Stray's eyes, full of sympathetic understanding, darted back to Cutter's face, but found his friend's expression unreadable. That Cutter was holding himself in such exquisite control spoke volumes. He handed Matrix over to his father, unable to say anything.

Matrix grinned happily at Steele, unaware of the tense situation. He gave him a kiss of greeting, and spoke with excited enthusiasm.

"There's Mommo! Hi, Mommo! Dodden-dee, look! Kids!"

Cutter followed the direction of his son's gaze, and realized that Matrix was referring to the greys. The innocent naiveté knifed into him. He swallowed hard.

"Matrix, want to go and play with those kids?" he asked over the lump in his throat.

His son looked at the greys surrounding the clearing, nodded eagerly, and smiled. "OK, Dodden-dee!"

* * *

He was so caught up in watching his son being carried away by the greys, that he was never even aware of Ennopy leaving with them. After an eternity of non-thought, the sound of Angel's anguish brought him back to his surroundings.

Stray had gone off to report everything to the home

world authorities, leaving them alone.

Angel sat on the ground where she'd collapsed, sobbing brokenly, as Cutter approached her. Her son was gone. The greys had taken her child.

"Angel. You know I had to--" Began Cutter, but the words caught in his throat when he spied the look of venom in her dark eyes.

"You goddamn son-of-a-bitch! What kind of a monster are you? You gave them our baby! I *hate* you!" And she broke down again, choking and crying.

"I know." he said. He pulled her to her feet, and she fell into his embrace, sobbing hysterically. He held her tenderly, his body shaking with the urgency to renew their hormonal bond. He ignored the temptation, and kissed her forehead gently, knowing instinctively that it would be for the last time.

She let him hold her for several long moments. At length, she stopped sobbing and pulled away to gaze steadily up into his pale, almost-white eyes.

"That day outside of Boomer's, you told me I'd never regret it, if I gave you a second chance. You've had that chance, and you were wrong. I'm leaving you."

He nodded. He'd known that too. She couldn't live with him now, after what he'd done. She couldn't love him, now that she knew exactly what kind of betrayal he was capable of.

* * *

As Angel walked away, Cutter felt himself sliding into another attack of withdraw spasms. He surrendered to the pain, less tortured by its agony than he was by her desertion. He gave himself to the extreme sensations washing over him, letting them drown the inner screams of his heart and soul.

The sound of the grey's ship launching brought him out of his haze of suffering, and he looked up just in time to see the alien ship slip smoothly over the Pennsylvania woodlands, the late afternoon sun glinting off its metallic body.

It was then, that the full impact of what he'd done registered on his awareness. His son was gone forever.

"You unfeeling bastards!" he screamed through

clenched teeth, shaking his fist at the sky in a futile gesture.

The flare of the retreating ship faded and died, and Cutter fell to his knees, gnashing his teeth and weeping for his son.

"Matrix! Oh . . . Matrix . . . my son . . . there was nothing else I could do . . . forgive me . . . "

* * *

"Where's Angel--?" Stray had returned from reporting to their superiors, to find Cutter alone by the cabin, in the lengthening shadows.

"Gone." The tortured finality in Cutter's voice told Stray that she wasn't coming back. Ever. So, then Cutter's sacrifice was three-fold. He'd not only lost his son, but his woman, and therefore his life as well. He'd wither and die without Angel. There was nothing Stray could say. No comfort he could give.

At long last Cutter broke the silence that had fallen between them.

He stirred, said, "She thinks I'm a monster, you know. A demon." he sighed, thinking of his son. "I don't know, maybe I am . . . "

"No demon would do what you've done. They came here in force and, rather than negotiate, gave us an ultimatum. You saved all of us with your sacrifice."

It was many long moments before he was able to control his voice enough to answer.

"But the price . . . was too high, Stray."

171

Chapter 21: The Saint and the Demon

Later, Present Day

"The greys kept their word. After the day they took my son, I never saw them or their crafts again."

A knock at the shanty door interrupted the old man's story. My editor had finally arrived to judge the validity of his incredible claims.

When Al's eyes lit upon the woman in the doorway, a sudden and severe burst of pain swept through him, a gut-wrenching agony that doubled him over on the bed. After a few moments, he unfolded and fell back onto the pillow, his features pale, and his whole body trembling. But his almost-white eyes burned with something indescribable, an intensity I hadn't seen before.

"Angel . . ." The name tore from his throat like a rusty nail out of wood. "What . . . are you doing . . . *here?*"

I was stunned. *Angel?* My editor, Laura Woodhouse, was *Angel?* Why hadn't I seen it? How could I have missed it? The shock was almost too much for the reporter in me. I wanted to ask her a hundred different questions, but I kept silent, watching the rest of the story unfold before me.

She moved to approach him, but he motioned her back. "Don't. You know what being near to you . . . does to me now . . . Is this, then, the final torture?"

"Cutter? Is it really you?" She knew it was; even I could tell that she knew. She said his name softly, with a deep reverence that immediately evoked an intense envy in me. If my former girlfriend had ever looked at me or spoken to me like that, we would have stayed together forever.

I realized then, that Angel must have been hunting for him all this time. She'd finally found him, here, in the middle of a Florida swamp.

She looked around the poor shanty, said, "This is where you've lived all these years?"

"It's not much," he admitted in a gravel voice. "But my needs are few."

She must have suspected the old man's identity for some time, and had sent me here, to the middle of this God-forsaken bog to make certain. I had been left out of the loop, and felt that I'd been unfairly used. She had sent me here--not for a story--but to confirm her suspicions.

Al seemed to have come to the same conclusion.

"I'm near my end . . . Is that what you'd hoped? Is that why you're here? To see me die?"

"Cutter, no." she choked on the words, then motioned to someone outside, and a tall, golden young man came to stand just behind her in the doorway. His skin was as dark as Angel's, but golden, like Al's, and his coarse, curly hair was a flaxen blond. But his most remarkable feature was his eyes. Pale, and almost white.

"Matrix?" Cutter's voice broke. Was this truly his son? He thrust his weakening Will at the boy in a flash of his brilliant pale eyes, and found it returned, stronger by far.

"Yes, Dodden." he replied, coming past her into the room. He came to the foot of the bed, where the light from the oil lamp lit his features, and his father could see him.

"Matrix, you must know why I--"

"I do know. Mommo knows as well. You saved her life. They would've killed her to get me. You knew they wanted me, knew they might not harm me. It was a risk you were willing to take."

"I had no right to risk you--"

"You had no choice. But your hopes were fulfilled. The greys understand us now. Through me. They've learned of our capacity for Love, and the sacrifices we're willing to make for it. They no longer have reason to fear our Talent. They've returned me as a sign of their new-found trust."

"Then, I . . . can die in peace . . . "

Al's words faded as he turned to me. He coughed harshly, then said, "You see, boy? It was always . . . a matter of . . . Love." He clamped his jaws together as his discomfort increased, and his trembling became violent. Even a fool such as I could see that he was running out of time. And I wondered at that moment, what Angel saw when she looked at him. Did she see the frail, desiccated shell before her, or did she see the strong, virile man he once was?

Angel spoke up again, answering my unspoken question.

"I kissed your pain away once, do you remember?"

"It wasn't so long ago, and I'm not so far gone, that I'd forget a thing like that. Of course I remember!" He grumped. His hands gripped the blankets, claw-like, but that didn't stop the tremors that wracked them.

"Let me try again, Cutter."

She wanted to renew their Bond, then? I wondered hopefully if it were possible. But he shook his head slowly.

"It's too late . . . I don't have the energy, Angel . . . "

"Even though I hated what you did, I never stopped loving you, Cutter."

"I know that . . . and I will love you . . . for all eternity."

"Then, at least let me stay. Let me try to make it easier for you."

Shuddering with pain and emotion, he relented, his eyes coming up to meet hers at last. Their gazes locked and held. I think he was no longer aware of Matrix and me. He held out a frail, shaking arm, and she went to him. Her tears fell onto the blanket as she bent over the old man and kissed him. It was a soft, lingering kiss that could have easily aroused a cadaver. I saw his features relax immediately. His quivering ceased and a look of relief and utter peace replaced the pain on his ravaged face.

I motioned to Matrix, and we left them to their privacy.

I had no idea whether or not they would be able to renew their Pair Bond, if she would be able to save Cutter, or whether he would die in her arms. I preferred to believe that their Love would conquer everything. That this man who had sacrificed and lost everything he had ever loved, would regain it all in the end.

As Matrix and I strolled away from the shanty, we began to talk. He was intelligent and well spoken. I asked him how--living among the nonverbal greys for six years--that it was possible. His answer was unexpected.

He said, "My tutor/translator, Ennopy. You wouldn't believe how much he's taught me!"

The irony of his reply was not lost on me. I must have smirked, for he said, "You seem bitter."

Me? Bitter? "And why not? Your mother sent me down here on an assignment, and I've wound up with nothing."

"But you got your story, didn't you?"

"HA! Nothing printable." Now that the greys had been gone for the past six years, no one would believe a word of what I'd write. There was no longer any evidence. The Resistance, with their ties to the FBI, had made sure of that. I said as much.

Matrix gave me a curious grin. "I've learned from Mommo that newspapers and magazines aren't the only outlets for writing. There's a lot of money to be made elsewhere."

I almost stumbled on a tussock of swamp grass. It had never occurred to me, that I could turn this tale into something more than the report I'd been sent to get. A *book*, perhaps?

We continued to converse, and I saw that this six-year-old teenager was wise and original in a way that no one else on this planet could be. A boy from two different worlds, who had lived on a third, and I realized that he, too, had a unique story to tell.

Perhaps he'd tell it to me.

Printed in the USA
CPSIA information can be obtained
at www.ICGtesting.com
LVHW021251310524
781674LV00013B/632